HOMEWARD

PROPERTY OF

_____

_____

J. P. MARTIN was born in Scarborough in 1879. He started telling the *Uncle* stories before the First World War and in 1932 the writers Stella Martin Currey and R. N. Currey urged him to write them down. Rejection after rejection followed for thirty years until they were accepted by Jonathan Cape in 1964. Reviewers welcomed each of the six books as they were published between 1964 and 1973 with comparisons to the poet Edward Lear and to Lewis Carroll; '. . . a classic in the great English Nonsense tradition' said *The Observer*.

J. P. Martin was eighty-four when *Uncle* was published and he charmed everyone on radio and television. He was able to enjoy his late success before he died in 1966.

The Uncle series by J. P. Martin

UNCLE

UNCLE CLEANS UP

UNCLE AND HIS DETECTIVE

UNCLE AND THE TREACLE TROUBLE

UNCLE AND CLAUDIUS THE CAMEL

UNCLE AND THE BATTLE FOR BADGERTOWN

THE COMPLETE UNCLE

J. P. MARTIN

UNCLE

Illustrated by Quentin Blake

PUFFIN BOOKS

UK | USA | Canada | Ireland | Australia
India | New Zealand | South Africa

Puffin Books is part of the Penguin Random House group of companies
whose addresses can be found at global.penguinrandomhouse.com.

www.penguin.co.uk
www.puffin.co.uk
www.ladybird.co.uk

First published by Jonathan Cape 1964
Reissued in this edition 2017
001

Text copyright © J. P. Martin, 1964
Illustrations copyright © Quentin Blake, 1964

The moral right of the author and illustrator has been asserted

Set in 12.5/16.5 pt Sabon LT Std
Typeset by Jouve (UK), Milton Keynes
Printed in Great Britain by Clays Ltd, St Ives plc

A CIP catalogue record for this book is available from the British Library

ISBN: 978-0-141-37922-7

All correspondence to:
Puffin Books
Penguin Random House Children's
80 Strand, London WC2R 0RL

MIX
Paper from
responsible sources
FSC
www.fsc.org   FSC® C018179

Penguin Random House is committed to a
sustainable future for our business, our readers
and our planet. This book is made from Forest
Stewardship Council® certified paper.

To James, Andrew, Alice, Judith, Matthew

Contents

Some of the Characters

Some of the Characters

THE BADFORT CROWD

Beaver Hateman
Nailrod Hateman (Sen.)
Nailrod Hateman (Jun.)
Filljug Hateman
Sigismund Hateman
Flabskin
Hitmouse
Mud-Dog
Oily Joe
Skinns
Crackbone
Hootman
Jellytussle

Abdullah the Clothes-
  Peg Merchant
Toothie
The Wooden-Legged
  Donkey
The Bookman
Ghosts
Etc., etc.

HATED BY BOTH
SIDES

Old Whitebeard

1. A Ride Round

UNCLE is an elephant. He's immensely rich, and he's a BA. He dresses well, generally in a purple dressing-gown, and often rides about on a traction engine, which he prefers to a car.

He lives in a house called Homeward, which is hard to describe, but try to think of about a hundred skyscrapers all joined together and surrounded by a moat with a drawbridge over it, and you'll get some idea of it. The towers are of many colours, and there are bathing pools and gardens among them, also switchback railways running from tower to tower, and water-chutes from top to bottom.

Many dwarfs live in the top storeys. They pay rent to Uncle every Saturday. It's only a farthing a week, but it mounts up when there are thousands of dwarfs.

There is one mysterious block in the middle called Lion Tower, which hardly anybody has been into. People have tried, but they get lost.

Exploring in Uncle's house is a tricky business, but there's one comfort, you are sure to come across something to eat, even if you have lost your way.

On the morning when this story starts, Uncle was waking in his room which looked out on to the moat.

His big bed was hung with red silk curtains, and they looked very grand in the morning sunlight.

In came the Old Monkey with a bucket of cocoa. He looks after Uncle very well because Uncle once saved him from a mean old stepfather who tried to sell him for sixpence. There are lots of other people who work for Uncle, but the Old Monkey is the chief one. They get on splendidly.

'Good morning,' said Uncle. 'Anything happening over at Badfort?'

He drew the cocoa up with his trunk, and squirted it down his throat, never spilling a drop.

'Everything seems quiet, sir,' said the Old Monkey, drawing the window curtains and picking up a telescope which lay on the sill. He focused it on a large ramshackle building about a mile away and reported: 'Beaver Hateman is just setting off for a ride on the Wooden-Legged Donkey, and Hitmouse is washing up.'

'Washing up, eh! They *are* peaceful,' said Uncle. 'It might be a good day for a ride round.'

'Oh yes, sir, let's go, sir,' said the Old Monkey, enthusiastically. There is nothing he likes so much as a ride round.

'Perhaps they're turning over a new leaf at Badfort,' said Uncle, the bed groaning and creaking as he got out of it.

The Old Monkey said nothing. He knew from past experience that this wasn't likely, but he put down the telescope.

'I'll go and get the ham ready, sir,' he said.

Uncle picked up the telescope as soon as the Old Monkey had gone and had a look at Badfort himself. It's rather hard when you have a splendid house yourself that the chief view from your windows should be that of your enemy's dingy fortress, but this had to be endured, and it's quite useless to pretend that Uncle wasn't interested in the huge sprawl of Badfort, and the unseemly Badfort crowd who inhabited it.

Since Uncle became rich the people who live at Badfort have been his chief critics. They are jealous of him, and are delighted when they discover anything against him. For instance, he used, when he was young, to find it difficult to tell the truth always, but he wasn't a very clever liar, because he couldn't help blowing softly through his trunk when he was telling a lie, and people got to know of this. Also he once borrowed a bicycle without permission when he was at the University, and, being rather heavy, broke it. People have long memories for such deeds in a great person.

It is hard to say who is the head of Badfort. Beaver Hateman is the most active person there, and he has two brothers called Nailrod and Filljug. Then there's a cousin called Sigismund Hateman. One of the most objectionable characters is Jellytussle. He is covered with shaking jelly of a bluish colour, and whenever he is about Uncle looks out for trouble. But perhaps it is safe to say that Hootman is the master spirit. Many people think he is a kind of ghost. Certainly he keeps in the background, but he works out many successful plots against Uncle.

Uncle looked with disapproval along the whole rickety length of Badfort, noting that there were more windows than ever stuffed with sacking. He changed the focus a little to look at the small Nissen hut outside the gate of Badfort. Yes, it was just as the Old Monkey had said. Hitmouse was washing up. Hitmouse, a little coward, who carried skewers as weapons, and who hated anybody else to be prosperous, lived a very untidy life. He had hundreds of cups and saucers, and he kept on using them till he had only a small place to sleep in near the door. When the muddle became unbearable he began to clean up.

'It may be a sign of trouble,' said Uncle thoughtfully.

Then he got on with his dressing.

There are no stairs from Uncle's room. Instead he takes a big slide which lands him in the hall. When he wants to go up there's a moving rope at the side. He can get hold of this with his trunk and it draws him up very quickly.

The Old Monkey was soon hard at work supplying him with hams. The Young Monkey came stumbling in with a net full of cabbage, but he is no good as a waiter. He stutters and shuffles about. When Uncle blows through his trunk he shakes like a jelly.

...cle, 'what's in the post this

'Just this,' said the Old Monkey. He handed Uncle a cheque for £1,000 for the sale of maize, and a gold elephant's trunk ring weighing three pounds.

'Ring up Cowgill,' said Uncle, 'and tell him to get the traction engine ready.'

Cowgill, the engineer, was once an enemy of Uncle's. He used to make splendid mechanical traps in the ground, and powerful steel catapults to discharge bags of ashes at him – a thing Uncle hated, for the ashes got up his trunk and spoilt his grandeur. However, that was a long time ago, and now all Cowgill's skill is at Uncle's disposal.

The traction engine was kept by him in first-class condition at his works, which are part of Uncle's house. It is painted red, but the big fly-wheel is polished brass. In front of the engine is a small brass elephant as a mascot. This is kept very bright, but someone from Badfort often succeeds in throwing mud over it. This makes Uncle furious, for he can't bear to see a spot on it. Uncle has a gilded armchair set among the coal, and there is a steam trumpet which makes a noise like an elephant. It's most thrilling to hear it.

Uncle, the Old Monkey and Cowgill set out.

'We'll call on Butterskin Mute on the way,' said Uncle.

Mute is the best farmer in the neighbourhood, and he supplies Uncle with fresh vegetables. He's a little, smiling man, and he sometimes wears spade boots. These boots have short spades attached to them for digging.

'What's the matter, Mute?' asked Uncle, thinking the little man looked low-spirited today.

'Beaver Hateman and some of the others have been over in the night and stolen my largest pumpkins,' said Butterskin Mute sadly. 'Including one – a very big one – I was saving for you.'

'Those miscreants shall not go unpunished,' said Uncle. 'Meanwhile, here is a bag of sugar, and a bag of coal from the traction engine to cheer you up. Now we must hurry on to Badgertown. We're lunching at Cheapman's today.'

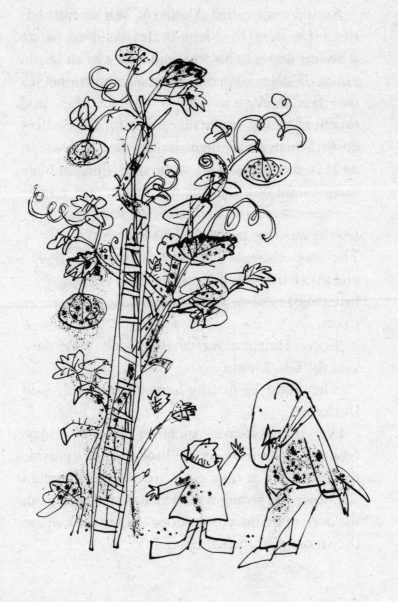

An old man called Alonzo S. Whitebeard has the farm next to Mute's. He has long white whiskers down to his feet, and he is a great miser. He has a silver sixpence as big as a millstone. It's two feet thick, and almost six feet high, and therefore almost impossible, even for the Badfort crowd, to steal. At night he sits and looks at it, and as they went past now they thought they caught sight of it through a window.

They neared the dark hulk of Badfort. On the way they passed Gaby's Marsh. The mud there is intensely sticky and infested by small savagely-biting fish called scobs. They are awful to eat.

'Beaver Hateman was catching scobs yesterday,' said the Old Monkey.

'They must be getting hard up for food,' said Uncle.

Everything seemed quiet at Badfort today. Nobody was sitting on the broken chairs outside the door, but as they got near, Beaver Hateman slid down the strong wire which is stretched from the door of Badfort to the door of Oily Joe's where they mostly do their shopping.

'He must have quarrelled with the Wooden-Leg,' said Uncle.

Beaver Hateman and the Wooden-Legged Donkey are always together, and always quarrelling, but today the Wooden-Leg had remained behind. Perhaps it was he who put on a comic gramophone record as they passed a broken window – 'Uncle Goes Fishing'. There was a yell of laughter, but Cowgill put on speed, and also blew the steam trumpet, and they got past without further incident.

Badgertown is a large flat place inhabited by badgers of the most simple and credulous nature. In the middle of the town there is a huge building known as Cheapman's Store. It's really a delightful place. You can get things there for next to nothing. Nearly all the badgers shop there.

Of course there are other shops, but they have a struggle. They get what customers they can by weeping at their doors and entreating people to come in. Of course they can buy their own provisions at Cheapman's, but that naturally goes against the grain.

'What's the special line at Cheapman's today?' asked Uncle.

'Motor-bikes only a halfpenny each, and flour at four sacks a penny,' said the Old Monkey with delight.

They went in, and Uncle ordered a half-penny lunch for himself, the Old Monkey and Cowgill.

'There are twenty-five courses, sir,' said the Old Monkey, 'and it will take about three hours to get through it.'

'Oh well,' said Uncle, 'we might as well have it; we haven't got a lot on today.'

At Cheapman's, instead of your tipping the waiter, *he* gives *you* a present. Today the waiter handed Uncle a parcel containing a sewing machine, seven pounds of chocolate and a very good brass trumpet.

'You can have the sewing machine,' said Uncle to the Old Monkey. 'It's a mystery to me how Cheapman makes his profits.'

But make them he did. Cheapman is almost as rich as Uncle, and far richer than the King of the Badgers, who lives in a tumbledown palace on the edge of the town, and frequently has to arrange for loans from Uncle to tide him over difficulties.

They returned home a different way, a pleasant route through a deep lane with high hedges, but Uncle does not like it much, because it's a noted place for what he calls treachery.

'Run through the lane and keep the hooter going!' he said to Cowgill.

The latter replied by putting on all steam and raising a deafening roar from the steam trumpet.

As they brushed through some thick bushes Uncle filled his trunk from one of the buckets he always keeps filled on the traction engine, just in case.

But nothing happened. They came out into the open unmolested.

'What's happened to the Badfort crowd?' asked Uncle testily. 'Are they losing their spirit or what? They've done nothing today!'

'Perhaps it's because you are going to give out bathing tickets this afternoon,' suggested the Old Monkey. 'Even the Badfort crowd like to go to the baths, sir.'

'Glad you reminded me,' said Uncle, feeling in the pocket of his dressing-gown for the bundle of tickets. 'I'd almost forgotten.'

Homeward looked magnificent as they rode towards it, the sun shining on its pink and green and blue towers. At the base of one, a train was unloading six thousand cases of oranges. They stopped to watch. This train backed out, and an equally long one came up loaded with pineapples. This had only just disappeared when another came whistling up loaded with sacks of raisins. Each sack was put into a kind of catapult and shot into a hatchway three storeys up. It was a very pretty sight.

When the Old Monkey blew a trumpet Uncle heard a shout from Beaver Hateman: 'Bathing tickets for tomorrow!' – and turned to see a strange crowd assembled.

All the Badfort crowd were there behaving very quietly for once. Whitebeard and his detestable stepfather were in the front. Flabskin was there positively blubbering for a ticket, Beaver Hateman was holding out his hand in a lordly way, and the Wooden-Legged Donkey held out his leg which has a small receptacle at the end for cash, tickets, etc.

'Do you think they ought to be allowed to go to the baths?' asked the Old Monkey anxiously.

'Oh, I think they might for once,' said Uncle, who was in a good humour after watching the fruit unloading. 'They've been almost polite today.'

Back at Badfort Beaver Hateman congratulated his followers on their good behaviour.

'We must plan for tomorrow,' he said. 'Some can be filling the water-polo ball with glue and ink and tin-tacks, and remember to rub it thin in one place just before you throw it at the Old Monkey. Others can be putting drawing-pins in their bathing suits. The rest can get lunch ready.'

'Wait until we get into those baths!' muttered Hitmouse. He began to foam at the mouth with a kind of green froth, a sure sign that he is getting jealous of Uncle.

2. Uncle's Baths

YOU will want to hear more about these wonderful baths that aroused such interest even among the hardened inhabitants of Badfort. They are situated right in the midst of a group of towers. It is impossible to find them without a guide; even Uncle does not know the way there. When he wants to go, he rings up on the telephone:

WASH-HOUSES 39485765764756

He has it written on a card because it's not very easy to remember. But the moment after he gets through, a strong dwarf called Titus Wiley appears, carrying a bunch of keys in a leather wallet. The bath passage is at the side of the front door. It's handy, but mysterious. There's just a small keyhole, and the door is opened with an ordinary-looking key. But try to open it without that dwarf, and you will find your mistake.

Nailrod Hateman has spent hours working at the lock, and the Old Monkey has had many a go out of curiosity, but it's no good. They have to wait for Titus Wiley.

When Uncle came out to go to the baths, a motley crew were lined up along the moat. Beaver Hateman was at the front, of course, and Whitebeard at the rear, nearly out of sight at the end of a string of badgers. He was occupying his time while they waited in trying to catch some fishes in the moat.

'Are you all ready to go?' said Uncle.

'Yes, we are, and hurry up!' said Beaver Hateman snappishly. Uncle looked at him sternly, and then said:

'Well, you can all turn round, and march round the tower keeping exact order; then the first to arrive at the other side will lead the way. And, mind you, no pushing! When the party arrives at the other side Alonzo S. Whitebeard will be in front and Beaver Hateman last!'

Beaver Hateman bubbled with rage, but he was so anxious to get into the baths that he curbed his temper, merely pinching Nailrod, who was next to him.

Then Titus Wiley unlocked the door, and the march began. The passage was badly lit, and there seemed to be some rough work going on, for every now and then you could hear a yell from the badgers who marched in front and chunks of limestone could be seen hurtling through the air. However, they progressed fairly well. All at once they came to a place where the passage began to show holes at the side. Then it doubled back on itself, and you could see through these holes that the front of the procession had turned and was now moving in the opposite direction.

Uncle stopped the march for a moment.

'Last time when we reached this stage on our journey,' he said, 'we had considerable uproar, owing to some miscreants throwing things through the holes at their advancing friends. Let this happen again, and the rear part of the procession will be headed round, and you'll all be marched out.'

This threat had a good effect, and the march continued in peace, except that Hitmouse tried to

singe Whitebeard's whiskers as they blew through
an opening.

Then, all at once, they drew up in a lofty
vestibule. Over a wooden door were some words
written on a card:

ENTRANCE TO BATH HOUSE

And, underneath, in small, neat handwriting:

*Any person objectionable in his conduct will be
refused entrance.*

Uncle pointed to these words with his trunk,
and said: 'You will perhaps understand my hesi-
tation in bringing you, when you read that!'

'Oh, shut up!' said Sigismund Hateman in a
gentlemanly voice. 'Really, I shall begin to wonder
if it's worthwhile coming to your old baths, if
you preach so much!'

This speech, however, was drowned in a chorus
of howling. Everybody was anxious to get in. And
here comes another mystery. These baths were of
huge extent, and yet, judging by the way they had
marched, they *must* be in the base of a small
tower, next to Uncle's dining-room. They have all

puzzled over this, but it's no use asking Titus Wiley. He simply grins, and says:

'There's a many things about baths, as people doesn't understand, as isn't employed there.'

All the same, it's a bit irritating to consider that this vast expanse of water is so placed that, humanly speaking, it can't be there.

At last Titus Wiley turned the key in the door, and they marched in, and for the moment all strife was over.

They emerged into a building so colossal that the end of it was only a dim shadow. At their feet was the bath, the water of a pinkish colour and very clear. The first thing to be seen was a gigantic human face carved out of stone, and about the size of a house. The mouth constantly ejected a stream of water ten feet broad. A good swimmer can swim up against the stream, and get inside the skull, where there is a large room with a path round it and swirling water for the floor. A ladder leads to a long stone room above with a water-chute down the nostrils. You just walk in at the side of the eyes, and are instantly caught by a stream of water, and forced out of the nostrils like a bullet.

Everybody had a go at this except Uncle, who is rather too big to go down the nostrils, so he

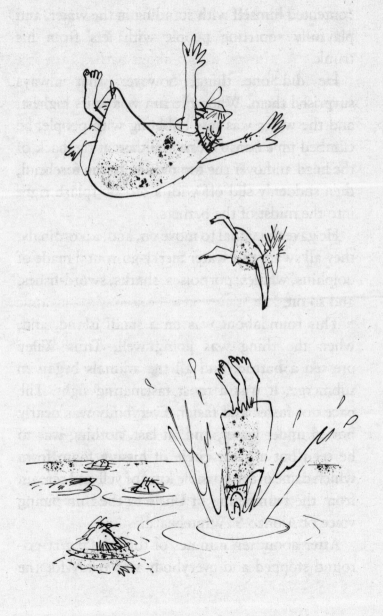

contented himself with standing in the water, and playfully squirting people with jets from his trunk.

He did one thing, however, that always surprised them. When the fun was at its highest, and the water was just bubbling with people, he climbed up a broad stone staircase at the back of the head and over the top of it on to the forehead, then suddenly slid off with a terrific splash right into the midst of the bathers.

He gave the signal to move on, and, accordingly, they all swam to a water merry-go-round made of dolphins, whales, porpoises, sharks, sword-fishes, and so on.

This roundabout was on a small island, and, when the thing was going well, Titus Wiley pressed a button, and all the animals began to submerge. It was a most fascinating sight. The pace got faster and faster. Everybody was nearly buried under water, and, at last, nothing was to be seen but a great circle of hissing foam from which came every possible kind of yell and scream from the trumpeting of Uncle to the thin piping voice of Alonzo S. Whitebeard.

After about ten minutes of this, the merry-go-round stopped and everybody was ready for the water-chutes. These were very fine. The biggest of them went up to such a height that the top was hidden in steamy mist.

By the side of the chute there was a kind of piston just projecting out of the water. People who sat on it were suddenly shot up towards the roof. When they got above the chute top they hovered and came gently to rest on the platform.

After the chute they had a go at the 'Skimmer', a thing like a sling that skimmed people over the surface of the water, just in the same way as a stone is skimmed. The Old Monkey won, making thirty-one dips.

By this time they were all ready for lunch, and Titus Wiley shouted:

'This way for the dining raft!'

This is a gigantic raft which goes round the baths while they have lunch. It's the only way to see the whole of the baths. It takes fully an hour to go round, and it does not move very slowly either.

On the raft was a huge pile of food: roast oxen, hams, dried goats' flesh, cartloads of bananas, casks of lemonade, as well as ginger-beer and other liquids. A great loaf of hay as big as a haystack stands in the middle, and a huge cake built like a castle with a passage through it. You walk through the cake, and cut slices with your knife.

When they had all eaten as much as they wanted, and the Badfort crowd had positively stuffed themselves, Uncle looked at his watch, and said:

'Time's up. Everyone must clear out!'

'Do you think we're going to leave this bath now?' said Beaver Hateman, going menacingly up to Uncle.

'Yes, I do!'

'Well, you're jolly well wrong! I'm going to stay here all night, if I want to!'

Uncle was about to reply when Titus Wiley pulled his sleeve, and began to whisper in his ear.

Uncle smiled and nodded, and immediately motioned to the Old Monkey to call out that it was time to go home. Most of them were soon on the bank, but the Hateman crowd were still in the water, and were beginning to produce bladders of vinegar and other objectionable weapons.

Uncle said nothing, but just as the Badfort crowd floated together for a moment to discuss tactics, Titus Wiley pressed a button, and immediately a very strong current rushed out of the bath wall, and began to drive them all before it.

In vain they struggled. They were carried, a shouting mass, to the other side of the bath. There a door yawned for them, and they were instantly washed down a culvert, and hurled, a yelling, gibbering horde, into the moat.

'That's got rid of them,' said Uncle gravely, and then, turning to Wiley:

'That's a splendid idea of yours!'

'Well, I've thought it out on many a long summer afternoon,' replied Wiley. 'I call it the "Whirlpool Chucker Out", and I think I can say as it's effective!'

3. The Challenge

A T about eleven o'clock next morning, Uncle was aroused from the perusal of a very interesting book on the secret passages of Homeward.

The Old Monkey, who had been anxiously scanning the plain with field-glasses, said:

'Here's Jellytussle coming!'

Uncle grunted and went to the front door.

Sure enough, that very repulsive creature was crawling across the moat bridge. Jellytussle looked nearly as big as Uncle, but this was quite deceptive, as he was mostly jelly. He had small glittering eyes, and a large slippery mouth. He came on, holding in one paw a small tightly-rolled piece of parchment.

When he came near he began to bow in the strangest manner, very slowly, and yet the quivering jelly gave him the appearance of haste.

Uncle looked on contemptuously at this display of false homage, and held out his hand for the parchment.

It was written in blood, and read as follows:

To Uncle, the arch-humbug, impostor and bully.

Yesterday your worst deeds were outdone. When you got us all spouted into the moat, you thought you had done something clever. Well, you've done yourself in by that foul, atrocious action. We give you three days in which to repent.

If at the end of that time you make your appearance at Badfort, with a bag containing a thousand gold pieces, and with a written apology in your hand, we will pardon you.

Otherwise, we shall attack your miserable old castle, and you yourself will know what it means to be imprisoned and publicly tortured.

We are signing this at midnight in our own blood. Our trusty messenger, Jellytussle, brings this.

We hope that we shall see him again alive, and if we don't, we shan't worry, as he's inclined to be too polite in giving his challenges.

BEAVER HATEMAN
NAILROD HATEMAN
FILLJUG HATEMAN
SIGISMUND HATEMAN
J. HAWKINS FLABSKIN
ISIDORE HITMOUSE
WILLIAM MUD-DOG
MALLET CRACKBONE
J. MERRYWEATHER OILER (OILY JOE)
H. SLIMEGROVE BINNS
JOSEPH SKINNS

And at the bottom, in thin, shadowy, spidery writing, Uncle could just make out the faint signature:

Firlon Hootman

Uncle said nothing, but he measured Jellytussle with his eye. He was going to kick him up. The Badfort crowd are tough and can stand being kicked, but they all hate being kicked up into the air.

He rushed at Jellytussle. There was a squelching thud and the body of the messenger could be seen rising in the air. He looked like an inflating balloon as strips of loose jelly floated round him. He sent out a thin piercing cry as he rose.

It was really a magnificent kick. Snatching up their field-glasses, Uncle's party saw the revolving body describe a stately arc, and then descend, slowly and majestically, into the very midst of the Badfort crowd who were feasting in front of Badfort.

Uncle was gratified to see that his missile had fallen right on to their plates, scattering their dinner and splashing them with hot gravy. Some ran about, clutching their scalded limbs. Some took out hating tablets and began to write methodically. At last, they all gathered together, lifted up their hands, and sent forth a fierce yell of defiance in the direction of Homeward.

Uncle smiled.

'Well, whatever happens,' he said, 'that was a first-class kick. I don't know that I've ever given a better. And now let them come. I know quite well that they won't attack me for some time, because they are out of weapons. They've been selling their crossbows and duck bombs to buy bottles of Black Tom, so we're all right for a bit. However, I

The rest of the afternoon I spent in a seething
muddled sort of ... on ... you could ... an
vision of ... which ... took. An infinite

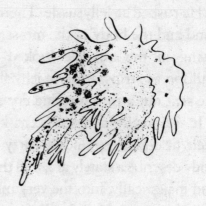

It ... ... standing up
right at ... ... my own the ears or
and much taller ... the very ... of the human

Crooks were never leaving it here of Feathers

Able was grabbed to see that his own field
slaves right on it their place, whether now
thinner and releasing their with her grey, some
rat skins, flicking their ... limbs, some
about not having chicken and beans, ... write

methodically. At last, they all seemed together
lifted up their hands, and stretched ... the rest of
drifted in the direction of ...

There ...

Well, whatever ... ...
tartest class talking from ... ... shrank
better. And new fortheir ... ... would
she has was either ... ...
They are out of meetings ... ... communicating
their elbows and ... ... of
Black Tony ... were ...

will just send a telegram to my brother Rudolph telling him to turn up.'

Uncle's brother is a celebrated big-game hunter, and he always comes over to help Uncle when he is in serious trouble with the Badfort people.

He is always glad to come, for fighting the Badfort crowd can be excellent sport, but it takes him some time to come, because he's always abroad.

However, on this occasion, Uncle soon got a wire back:

```
HAVING UNPRECEDENTED SPORT IN WOLFLAND,
BAGGED NINETEEN MUSK-OXEN AND THIRTY-
NINE GRIZZLIES. COMING AT ONCE. DO NOT
MEET ME AT BADGERTOWN. RUDOLPH
```

'Ah, he's coming to one of the other stations,' said Uncle. 'Now, we have a day or two before he comes. I've told Cowgill to prepare some vinegar squirts. Have the windows been well rubbed with Babble Trout Oil?'

Babble Trout Oil is a special preparation made from the babble trout, a small fish, difficult to catch. It renders glass tough, so that it is impervious to crossbow bolts and other missiles. Uncle often has his lower windows rubbed with it when trouble is threatening.

'And now,' said Uncle, 'I think we may as well do a little visiting in the towers. I think we'll call on the Old Man and Eva, and then go right up to the top of Lion Tower to call on Captain Walrus.'

The Old Man and Eva live at the top of Homeward Tower. They make medicines for a living.

Only Uncle and the Old Monkey went on this trip, and they took nothing with them but sandwiches. They got into an express lift at the end of the hall, and were soon whizzed up the two hundred storeys.

There was a big field at the top, and some gardens. In the middle of the field was a small house, with a sign which completely covered one side of it:

THOMAS CLATWORTHY SPENCER LIBERTAS
SWEETWATER CLANJOHN BREWAGE
TEMPLETON JOYCE GLEAMHOUND

His real name is Mr Gleamhound, but he is nearly always called 'the Old Man'.

On the other side of the house was another sign:

PURVEYOR OF DRUGS. PROPRIETOR OF
GLEAMHOUND'S HEADACHE MIXTURE,
GLEAMHOUND'S HEADACHE PRODUCER
(FOR ENEMIES), GLEAMHOUND'S HAIR
TONIC, GLEAMHOUND'S HAIR REMOVER,
GLEAMHOUND'S FAT REDUCER,
GLEAMHOUND'S FATTENING MIXTURE
FOR THE THIN, GLEAMHOUND'S
STOMACH JOY, ETC. ETC.

They are all very good, but they act the wrong way. For instance, his Headache Mixture gives you a frightful headache, his Jumbo Bunion Destroyer is well calculated to rouse bunions on a perfectly healthy foot. His Jacob's Well Eye Salve can put your eyes out of action for weeks, whereas his Punishment Eyesight Irritant (for enemies) will often cure people who have had to wear glasses for years.

Sitting in the house was Mr Gleamhound. He was perfectly bald, and wore immensely strong glasses over his inflamed eyes. He had been using his own hair restorer and eye salve for years.

Sitting on a low chair at his feet was Eva. Nobody seems to know her other names. She has always been with the Old Man, and he seems quite dependent on her.

'How are you getting on, Gleamhound?' said Uncle, carelessly seating himself on a bench.

'Oh, very well, very well indeed! After two thousand five hundred and eighty experiments, I have at last succeeded in making a nail-biting cure that is satisfactory.'

He glanced back as he spoke into his laboratory. It was large; in fact it seemed to take up almost the whole of the house.

On a blackboard, they could see chalked:

EXPERIMENT 2978

Mix mortar with arrowroot, and boil with gum mastic.

(*Unsuccessful*)

EXPERIMENT 2979

Boil shavings of parrot's bill with chopped hair and peroxide.

(*Unsuccessful*)

EXPERIMENT 2980

Boil Arnica and Lime in equal parts for the third of a day; thoroughly souse with rinsings from an old nitre vat, then pour in one oz. Peppermint, reduce to a jelly, and with great speed whirl in a hot aluminium pan, taking care to avoid direct sunbeams.

Then, lightly rub in flaked rice, ginger, rhubarb and orris root, in the proportions of $6 - 31\frac{3}{8} - 9$ and $27\frac{1}{8}$, at the same time shaking in equal proportions of boiled candy and lemon curd.

Repeat thirty-one times.

(*Successful!!*)

Uncle congratulated him and bought a bottle of Indigestion Producer (for enemies) and also a bottle of Stomach Joy, which was *supposed* to cure all forms of indigestion.

Then he took his leave, depositing, as he did so, five shillings on the table.

The Old Man's weary eyes gleamed, and he immediately shut up the laboratory for the day, and departed with Eva to Cheapman's Store, where they had a famous lunch, and departed at closing time with a well-filled truck of provisions and with threepence of the five shillings gone for ever.

Meanwhile, Uncle was proceeding to the very top of Lion Tower. He paused on the way to the elevator, and looked in at a small Post Office, from where he dispatched the bottle of Stomach Joy to Beaver Hateman.

'That'll give him something to think about,' he said, 'and, as I've been feeling a little groggy, I'll just take a spoonful of the Indigestion Producer (for enemies) now.' He did so, and gave one to the Old Monkey, and they both felt warm and braced.

Then they got into the elevator and after about ten minutes they got out at Summit Station.

Summit Station is at the very top of Lion Tower. It is so high that the whole tower bends in the wind. However, Captain Walrus lives at the top of a still smaller tower called Walrus Tower, which stands like a pencil at the edge of Lion Tower, and, if Lion Tower bends in the wind, Walrus Tower positively seems to flap to and fro when there is a gale. But this does not worry

Captain Walrus. He actually lives in the top storey of a very slender lighthouse at the top of Walrus Tower, and, rough old sea-dog that he is, he seems really to enjoy the sensation of constant swaying.

He is a staunch friend of Uncle's, and when he heard that there was likely to be trouble with the Hateman crowd, he cheerfully rubbed his hands.

'It's high time those swabs had a lesson!' he said. 'I thought something might be in the wind, so I've been getting ready a few extra marlinspikes. Call upon me when you want me, and in the meantime I'll keep a close watch on them through the glasses.'

Uncle thanked him for his help, and after a short talk they went back, because the lighthouse swayed so very much that they were in danger of being sick, in spite of the strengthening tonic they had taken on the way.

4. The Muncle

UNCLE always gets a lot of letters, but the Old Monkey does not often have one. However, next day he got one that filled him with joy.

'Oh, sir,' he said, 'my uncle is coming to see me!'

The Old Monkey's uncle is called the Muncle and he's a very nice person, but seems to live for footwear. Uncle likes him, but thinks he is a bit too fussy about shoes.

However, he told the Old Monkey that the Muncle would be welcome, and, about half an hour later, just as he had settled down to his paper, the Muncle arrived. He was wearing an enormous pair of travelling boots. These have electric motors in their soles so that they can run

along with him, and they come up so high that he can lean on the top edges. He always keeps a lot of stuff in them, including several pairs of smaller boots and shoes.

He came scooting over the drawbridge with an anxious expression, then drew up with a joyous shout. 'Not a spot of mud on them!'

He is always terribly afraid, when he comes to visit Uncle, that Beaver Hateman, the leader of the Badfort crowd, may splash his boots with mud. Beaver Hateman always tries to. But today he had seen nothing of him.

He sat down by the open window with a smiling face.

'So glad to see you, sir, and also my nephew. He looks well, though I am sorry to see his shoes are dusty. Nephew, open the right-side compartment in my travelling boots and you'll find a pair of dove-coloured visiting shoes. Ah, that's a relief. My travelling boots are rather heavy.'

Then he looked keenly at Uncle and said: 'Excuse my saying so, sir, but your shoes are somewhat shabby. I wonder if you'd gratify me by putting on a really nice pair?'

Uncle said to the Old Monkey:

'Just look in my number eight shoe saloon, and on the fourth shelf to the left you'll find a pair of red ones; I rather think it's the sixty-ninth pair from the door. Bring them here.'

The Muncle seemed deeply impressed by this speech. He had never imagined that even Uncle possessed such a vast stock. He was still more deeply moved when the Old Monkey appeared with an exquisitely shaped pair of elephant's morning shoes of a deep red colour.

'Oh, those look very well, sir!' he cried, in a rather envious voice. He was thinking hard how he might regain his lost ground as a shoe expert.

Then his face brightened, and he drew some papers from his pocket.

'These verses,' he said, 'were written by our local poet, and I thought so highly of them that I had a hundred copies printed. There's one for each of you, and perhaps my nephew wouldn't mind reading the poem aloud. I know you are fond of poetry, sir.'

As a matter of fact Uncle is not very fond of poetry, as he is everlastingly having it spouted at him by friend and enemy alike, but he resigned himself to the hearing.

The Old Monkey began to read in a low, well-modulated voice:

THE FOOT-LOVER
or
A Well-Spent Day

When in the morn he waketh
His *shoes* are all his care;
He heedeth not his jacket
As on them he doth stare.

Down the deep stairs he falleth;
For pain he does not care,
For on his *back* he landeth,
His *shoes* are in the air!

He hath a pleasant breakfast,
His well-brushed *shoes* are there;

His bacon tastes like nectar
As on them he doth stare.

At last he starts for business,
His eyes are on his *feet*,
Then the wrong bus he catcheth,
And reacheth the wrong street.

It went on, verse after verse, all about shoes.

When the poem was finished, Uncle sat still for a long time.

'Well, what do you think of it?' said the Muncle eagerly.

'I think as a poem it's moderately good,' replied Uncle, 'but I also think you are going too far in your craze for shoes. Shoes are good things, but we should not make them the *sole* object of life.'

Here he was interrupted, as a shadow fell upon them from the window.

Standing there was a great hulking man wearing a suit made of a sack with holes in it for arms and legs.

One look was enough.

It was Beaver Hateman.

'How do, Uncle!' he said. 'I see you've got the Muncle here. I nearly got him on the way. He just slipped past in time, or I'd have splashed his precious boots for him all right. However . . .'

He gave a loud whistle, and two of his friends who had been concealed in the ivy around the window suddenly rushed out with buckets of mud and threw them like lightning over the shoes of Uncle and his visitor.

'After them!' shouted Uncle, filling his trunk with water from a jug on the sideboard.

Uncle thundered over the drawbridge.

'Watch the bank!' he shouted.

Would you believe it, the miscreant came into view just at Uncle's feet, where he least expected him, and dashed into the bushes at such a rate that it was impossible to overtake him.

'We might as well give it up, sir,' said the Old Monkey. He was secretly laughing because Uncle had fallen over a tree trunk, and one tusk was fast in the ground. He got it out after a while, and with much trumpeting and blowing made his way back to the house.

'All right, Mr Hateman,' he muttered, 'I will remember this, and your punishment shall be swift and sure!'

They found the Muncle in very low spirits. 'My visiting boots are ruined!' he said in a sad voice.

'That's all right,' replied Uncle. 'Give him a new pair from the store,' he told the Old Monkey. 'And now, to take my mind off this disgraceful episode, I'll just look through the second mail, which I see has come.'

Uncle began to comfort himself by counting over the cash that had come in that morning. There was only a cheque for £2,570 for the sale of maize. He looked at it rather gloomily, and said to the Old Monkey:

'Not much cash in this morning. What are the expenses for the day?'

The Old Monkey is really very quick. He had it all written out on a small wooden board that he keeps by his chair.

Foodstuffs	£150
Ironmongery	15
Laundry	12
Wages of Staff	1
Total	£178

'That's too much!' said Uncle quickly. 'You must cut something down.'

However, he gave the Old Monkey £178 0s. 0½d. The halfpenny was a present and he thankfully pocketed it.

You'll think that Uncle's wage bill was small, but you must remember that everyone gets presents as well. Uncle pays very few people more than a halfpenny a week, but still it's a very good thing to work for him. He thinks nothing of giving every one of his staff a hundredweight of butter or twenty hams. They are all pretty well off, and the Old Monkey is positively rich. Besides his stores of tinned foods he has whole boxes full of clothes and books, and about twenty gramophones.

5. A Journey to the Oil Tanks

UNCLE looked at his watch after breakfast next day, and then consulted a great red calendar that hangs on the wall over the fireplace.

'It's about time I went to see the oil lake again,' he said. 'I'd like to fit in a visit before anything happens at Badfort.'

The Old Monkey's eyes brightened. He likes this expedition very much, because it's rather out of the ordinary.

So they soon gathered up their things, and started off. They only took the One-Armed Badger with them this time, because it's a dangerous place, and they don't want any people with them who are likely to fool about and cause trouble. The One-Armed Badger is an excellent worker, everlastingly scrubbing things. He is trustworthy and good at carrying blankets, baskets of buttered biscuits, bottles of meat extract, etc.

You pass through a little doorway in Uncle's kitchen when you want to go to the oil lake.

The kitchen is huge, partly underground, and all in the charge of the little dwarf, Mig. There's a great roasting fire on one side, which lights up the whole place, but most of the cooking is done on the oxy-acetylene gas stove. This oxy-acetylene burner is so hot that it can melt iron like butter. The consequence is that Mig can boil a kettleful of water in a second. He stands on the gas stove to work and wears dark glasses, or else the glare would ruin his eyes.

The way to the oil lake is just behind the stove. The stove runs out from the wall on rails, and behind it you see the opening of a passage.

But, when you're in, you are still confronted with difficulties.

There are seven steel doors to unlock, each one with a very complicated set of keys, and between each door is a short passage paved with very slippery round stones.

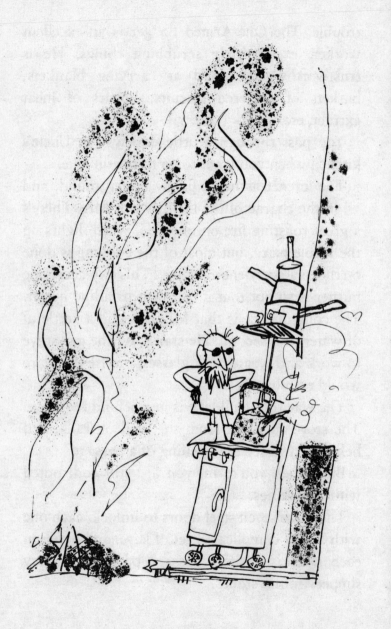

When you have passed through the last door, however, it's pretty easy. You just slide down a well-oiled slope to the lake.

Uncle likes to do this very quietly, because then he can see what the man who looks after the lake is doing. They slid down very gently, and glided along the margin. The lake is huge in size and very charming to look at, although it's underground, because it's lit up by thousands of electric bulbs of all colours.

Uncle knows just where the man who watches the lake can be found.

'That's the place,' he said. 'Round that craggy corner.'

When they got near the corner, Uncle crept forward and peeped round the cliff. Then he motioned to the Old Monkey to come to his side.

This is what they saw.

In front of them a barge was moored in the lake. Sitting in it, smoking a large cigar, was a little dark oily man. By his side there was a basket of fruit and nuts. He was reading an evening paper.

'Smoking!' hissed Uncle to the Old Monkey in a tense whisper. Just as he spoke, the little man,

finding that the cigar had gone out, lit it again with a match, and actually threw the match into the oil lake.

That was enough for Uncle. With a loud trumpet of rage, he turned the corner, and charged down towards the lake. The moment the little man heard him he thrust the cigar out of sight like lightning. At the same time he hid the fruit, and commenced to pull very hard on a rope, calling out as he did so the words of a heaving song:

'AH, EETCHA, EETCHA, E E T C H A A-H!' With every 'eetcha' he gave a tug at the rope.

Uncle, however, was not deceived by this display of energy.

He called out to him loudly:

'Guzman, bring that barge into shore at once!'

Guzman is the name of the man; he claims to be a Don, or Spanish gentleman, from Andalusia. He says he lost all his money by speculating in silver foxes; and he's working for Uncle till he gets enough money to retire. He speaks English with rather a rough accent, as he learned it at a sailors' lodging house near the docks when he landed penniless in England many years ago.

The Don sulkily pulled the barge to shore.

'You were smoking,' said Uncle testily.

Uncle is very much against smoking on the oil lake, because it's extremely likely that one day the whole place will catch fire. Now Guzman is a thoroughly good oil watcher in every other way, and looks after the lake well, but he *will* smoke, and this makes Uncle very doubtful about keeping him.

'Good morning, sir,' said the Don respectfully.

'You were smoking on the barge!' said Uncle sternly. 'I saw the cigar!'

'Cigar!' replied Guzman incredulously. 'You must be wrong. It's a reflection on the oil! I often sits watchin' the oil, and when there's a bit of an eddy, it takes all shapes, looks like a barrel or a jug, but specially like a cigar. Often I've said to myself, as I've watched 'em, "That's a cigar!" and then I've seen it melt away and vanish in the stream.'

'Liar!' said Uncle fiercely, and then, pointing to the oil: 'Look at all those dead matches! Why, you madman, you've actually been throwing matches into the oil!'

The Don looked staggered. At last he said: 'Well, I don't see the harm of an occasional smoke, sir. It gets a bit dull down 'ere continually watchin' the oil. Now, when I was at home in Andalusia, I 'ad my man ter waken me in the morning just as you 'ave, and 'e used ter sing a song as 'e 'ad made. It went like this:

'*Don Guzman, Don Guzman, I call you to the meal;*
Don Guzman, Don Guzman, the price is but one real;
There's hot baconario, and bread and buttario,
Besides a cupario of tea,
So get up your couragio, eat up your poragio,
And feast in the estancia with me!

'Now, I think you'll admit, sir, that after a life of that kind, I need some little solace here!'

Uncle began to relent. It's always the same with the Don – he talks Uncle round.

Soon they were quite friendly again.

The Don talks about his hardships, but after all he doesn't have a bad time. If ever he wants to get away from the lake, he has only to press a button in the wall on the opposite bank, and he finds himself in a cool green meadow at the foot of some gigantic tower.

After a while the Don looked at his watch and said: 'I vote we 'ave breakfast; it's half past two!'

It's a funny thing about the Don, he always breakfasts at this time.

As they went in Guzman said: 'Now, I've got a old custom as I 'ope you won't mind observin'. I pays for my own meals, and any guests as comes usually doesn't mind dubbin' up a real or so.'

He looked up doubtfully as he said this, but Uncle nodded carelessly, so he was reassured.

After a bit, his servant Gaberonez began to sing in the dining-room. It was the song that Guzman had recited to them; he had not mentioned that he still had a servant when speaking of his hardships.

They all walked into the dining-room.

On the table was a large money-box, labelled:

FUND FOR RETIREMENT TO ANDALUSIA.

Uncle dropped in a pound note, and a shilling each for the Old Monkey and the One-Armed Badger, while Guzman himself contributed a real.

The breakfast was a capital one, except for the porridge which was lumpy and sour, but the Don insisted that they should have some, as that was how people liked it in Andalusia. After that, the meal was faultless. The bacon was crisp and plentiful, and so was the toast.

As they sat down in the lounge, nourished and refreshed, Uncle said: 'I say, old chap, that money-box seems pretty full; I should think you have nearly enough to retire to Andalusia.'

'Oh, some day, some day,' replied the Don carelessly. 'It's not so bad here, and you must admit that I do the job well. I watch the tank from mornin' to night, and it takes some watchin'. Take them dwarfs now! They're always gettin' in through a place where there's a crack in the wall. They carries jugs with 'em, and tries to sneak the fluid. But I comes up softly, and bangs their jugs on their little bald 'eads. That settles 'em for the time.'

Uncle applauded this display of zeal, and then the Don said:

''Ow would yer like to go for a pull on the lake?'

'Very much indeed,' said Uncle.

They got into the barge, which was pulled across the lake by a rope. Uncle noticed Gaberonez did all the pulling while the Don sat dreamily in the stern chanting an old Spanish work song which he interpreted as meaning:

> *Pull, slaves, pull!*
> *Our souls are in the rope!*
> *One day we shall pull, pull, pull,*
> *Till the rope breaks.*

They reached the other side and got out.

After the somewhat stuffy atmosphere of the oil lake they all felt the need of a little fresh air, so they said goodbye to Don Guzman and looked round for a new way home.

They were wondering which direction to take when the Old Monkey found a kind of fire-escape, stretching both up and down the outside of a tower as far as they could see.

Uncle tossed a penny for choice of route. It fell down the ladder, and was immediately snatched by a dwarf who was looking out of a window.

'That means we go up,' said Uncle.

After going up about twenty flights of massive iron stairs, they came out on the top of an immense lonely tower. It had a perfectly flat top, without a rail of any kind, and looked very wind-swept and unsafe. At the very edge a huge fire was burning, and beside this lounged a couple of leopards. One of them was resting so carelessly that part of his body was actually hanging over the abyss. It looked awful, for down below you could see rows and rows of windows getting smaller and smaller, and at the very bottom a railway train that looked like a toy. The two leopards were cooking a large joint of pork over the flame. A little of the gravy kept running down

the wall, to be licked up by a dwarf leaning out of a window below.

Uncle asked them the price of a share.

They consulted together for a bit, and then one of them came up touching his cap.

'Two bob a slice, sir,' he said.

'Two bob!' said Uncle, blowing through his trunk. 'I'll give you a penny, and no more!'

They were about to refuse, but the Old Monkey whispered to them for a moment.

'Well, sir,' one of them said, 'it's rather hard on poor blokes like us, but you shall have it for a penny . . . and if you feel like making us a little present . . .'

Uncle smiled, and he gave them two large baskets of buttered biscuits, a coil of rope, seven bottles of meat extract, and a tin of Magic Ointment. They were specially glad to have this, because one of them had a sore paw, and the other one had a sick wife who had injured herself by falling off a tower.

By this time the sun was setting, and Uncle wanted to get back. Before they went they walked to the other side of the tower and looked over. Far below they saw Homeward Tower looking very small. Then came the moat and some fields and then the vast bulk of Badfort.

Uncle got out his telescope and looked through it.

'I can see Beaver Hateman, Nailrod Hateman, Sigismund Hateman, Flabskin and the Wooden-Legged Donkey, all sitting in a circle and drinking Black Tom,' he muttered.

'Can I have a look, sir?' asked the Old Monkey.

'No,' said Uncle severely, without taking the telescope from his eye. 'You don't want to look at those disgraceful hounds! Let's go home another way,' he added. 'I'm not going to climb down all those ladders again.'

'Begging your pardon, sir,' said one of the leopards, 'if you want to get to Homeward, the best way is to use the iron dive.'

'What's that?'

'Come here, sir.'

He led them to another side of the tower.

'You just jump off here one at a time, and you fall on an iron platform that springs.'

'But are you sure that it's safe?'

'Sure? . . . Why, I'm going that way home myself, so I'll make the first dive. It's balanced on hairsprings at the top, then bigger springs, then bigger ones still. You bounce a bit, but it soon settles. I'll show you. Just make a bundle of my share of the pig and buttered biscuit, and throw it after me,' he added to his companion.

He took the dive, turning over and over in the air. After he had fallen about a hundred storeys he struck the platform, which gave way and then sprang back. He bounced for a bit, and then they heard a faint roar from below which showed that he was all right. His goods were flung after him. He gathered them together and slunk off the platform, so they concluded that it would be safe to try the dive.

'You'd like to go first, sir?' said the Old Monkey.

'No, you can go.'

The Old Monkey took the jump, and seemed to take a long time to fall. However, he signalled that he was all right.

Then Uncle took the plunge. He hit the platform with a great clanging noise, bumped heavily, and then came to rest.

'I say,' he said to the Old Monkey, 'we must do this again; it's grand. We'll come here another day soon.'

They all agreed that it was a splendid sensation. There was a useful little railway at the foot of the tower on which they ran home in about ten minutes.

That evening Uncle was in such good spirits that he treated everyone to roast turkey and sausage, and he also gave them all good presents. They had six tins of fruit each for one thing, and Uncle also gave the Old Monkey a good suit of clothes and a handbag.

So they all went cheerfully to bed.

6. Miss Maidy and Dr Lyre

THERE were two more things Uncle wanted to do before Rudolf arrived. One was to inspect Dr Augustus Lyre's school of which he is a Governor, and the other was to visit an aunt of his who lives near the top of the highest tower, called Afghan Flats. Her name is Miss Evelyn Maidy, but she is always called Auntie.

So he set out, taking a few presents with him: a sack of tinned tongues, and a box of oranges. They were carried very willingly by the One-Armed Badger, who also insisted on stacking a suitcase on the top of them, with bandages, ointment, lamps and spare rations, and some socks for Uncle, in case his feet got tired.

The Old Monkey was there, of course, and the little kitchen dwarf Mig and the Muncle.

'What time shall we get to Dr Lyre's school?' asked the Old Monkey eagerly. 'I want to see if that old man Noddy Ninety who works on the tube trains is really there. He dresses up as a boy, sir, and goes to school for fun.'

'We'll have a cup of tea with Auntie and go straight afterwards,' Uncle promised.

They went up in the spiral lift. This is rather like an ordinary lift, but it keeps going round and round. It's very handy for going up a high tower. It never stops, but it slows down when it reaches the storey you want, and you just step off.

Afghan Flats is not in a very nice neighbourhood. It's full of thousands of dwarfs of the most cross and irritable disposition. You'll wonder why Auntie lives there. I'll tell you. It's because she loves domineering over the dwarfs, and I really believe they like having her there, though they are always having disputes.

Her lady companion is called Miss Wace. When Uncle reached Auntie's street, he asked a dwarf, who was eating a lemon, if he knew which was her house.

'You're her nephew, are you? You look like her – self-important.'

Uncle moved towards him menacingly, but he slipped down a side passage.

After a while they came to a very neatly-painted door. On it was a plate:

MISS MAIDY AND COMPANION

They knocked, and the Companion opened the door. She seemed weak and helpless.

'Oh, sir,' she said, 'this *is* good of you. I'm sorry that Miss Maidy is just lying down; one of those wretched dwarfs upset her just now!'

Just as she said these words, another door opened, and Auntie appeared. She had a big bruise on her forehead, but it was rapidly disappearing under the influence of a tin of Magic Ointment, which she held in her hand.

'So glad to see you, dear!' she said.

Uncle doesn't like to be called 'dear', but he has to put up with it.

Uncle motioned to the door, and the Old Monkey led in the One-Armed Badger, who shuffled clumsily along, almost hidden under the great orange-box and other things that he was carrying.

'A few presents for you,' said Uncle.

'Oh, that's very good. I'm always short of fruit, and there isn't a decent shop about here.'

'Well, why don't you go to Cheapman's?'

'Oh, Cheapman's is all right, but the trouble is *getting* there. I suppose I shall have to stick to the wretched little shop at the corner of the street. I've had great trouble with the proprietor, a miserable dwarf called Rugbo.'

At that moment, there was a knock at the door, and a shout: 'MILK O.'

Auntie jumped up, her headache forgotten.

'Excuse me a minute, I've just got to settle with this horrible little man. Last time he put a frog in the milk!'

She clutched her umbrella firmly, and went out. Next minute, they heard the noise of a heavy blow, followed by hissing and screeching.

'Now, that's done it!' said the Companion. 'She'll come back streaming with milk, and as weak and nervous as a kitten, and I shall have the job of calming her feelings.'

Uncle said nothing. He is used to his Aunt's curious ways, so he settled down comfortably in a chair, and had a look round the room, which is hung with diplomas. Auntie has won many prizes for ju-jitsu and wrestling; though in actual life she appears to do everything with her umbrella.

Just as he was looking at these things, they heard footsteps, and Auntie stepped in, humming a tune.

'Just give me a rub down, Wacy,' she said.

'How did you get on?' asked the Companion eagerly.

'Oh, very well, very well indeed. I don't think he'll try his tricks again for a bit. I pushed him into the non-stop lift. It only goes up and down once a day, so he's off for a bit, unless he likes to climb six hundred flights of stairs.

'Well, dear, I've been neglecting you,' she said, smiling at Uncle, 'and the Old Monkey. He's a dear! I really envy you the Old Monkey. Get the tea, Wacy.'

The Companion soon had a very choice meal set out, and Auntie seemed glad to exchange a little news.

'You seem to have all the luck, dear,' she said. 'We hear about your grand times, your thousands of cartloads of good things and cheques for maize. I don't know how you do it! I'm hard up myself. The wear and tear of things is incredible up here. Six chairs smashed yesterday, and the whole of my larder cleared out again! I'm sure I try to help the dwarfs, but they are so sly and cunning.'

They listened to some of Auntie's gramophone records after tea and then took the switchback to Dr Lyre's school.

Warm and glowing they alighted on a green, and were confronted by a long low set of rooms on the bottom storey of a massive tower. There was a rookery twenty storeys up, and some ravens seemed to have nested on a ledge thirty storeys higher still, while right at the top a pair of majestic eagles were slowly circling. A board was hung at the door.

DR AUGUSTUS LYRE
Select School for Young Gentlemen

Dr Lyre has an unfortunate name. His real name is simply 'Liar'. That's how you spell it, and he can't change it because he has had money left him on that condition. He usually spells it 'Lyre' – only sometimes he forgets, being absent-minded, and signs his letters 'A. Liar', and this amuses the boys very much.

When Uncle's party entered the schoolhouse, they found it somewhat dark, but a very pretty place. The lamps, though dim, were pink and orange, and the desks were made of blocks of polished cast iron, and shone with many reflections.

The Doctor was sitting in a large railed-in desk-compartment at one end, and the room was so long that it must have been hard for him to see the boys in the back rows. But the room was full of underground passages. If a boy wanted to see the Doctor, he dived into a hole by his desk, walked along a passage, and came up a short flight of steps near the Doctor's desk.

The Doctor has a bundle of great canes by his desk, and a thing like a flail, which he slaps down on his desk with a noise like thunder.

He seemed glad to see Uncle, for Uncle is the chairman of his Board of Governors. He called some of the senior boys to read aloud. They are not allowed to do this until they reach the top form, and then they do it all the time and all together.

They were reading a book written by the Doctor himself about the history of Lion Tower; that's the huge tower in the middle of Homeward, which has never been fully explored. According to the Doctor it was built in 1066, and that's one date every boy has to learn, or he can't get his GCE According to Uncle the tower was built by Wizard Blenkinsop only twenty years ago, and some of the boys know this and say that the Doctor's book is all wrong. But when they want to put him in a good temper, they all shout together '1066! 1066!' and that makes the old man purr.

When Uncle visits the school the Doctor turns to a page in the book where it describes the day on which Uncle visited Lion Tower and erected 144 drinking fountains for the dwarfs. That's in the modern history section, on page 11,564, only three pages from the end of the book. It's a big book, and expensive, but you've got to buy a copy or you can't get your GCE.

Uncle walked quietly to the back of the schoolroom, for he wanted to see if Noddy Ninety was there that day.

Yes, there he was. The Old Monkey knew him at once. What a spectacle! Imagine an old man of ninety disguised as a schoolboy of ten. He was wearing a little grey flannel jacket, and had a flaxen wig on his bald head.

Noddy Ninety loves to get into the bottom form and pretend he's a schoolboy. Then he has an easy time, because he knows the work, and also he seems to enjoy making himself a nuisance. He's had ninety years' experience of every school-boy trick imaginable, from putting tacks on seats to throwing ink.

He has more than twenty-five ways of stealing boys' lunches, and as for stealing caps and mufflers, well, they mostly keep them on, or they're gone at the end of the afternoon. He has been expelled from the school time and time again, yet he worms his way in again so cunningly that it's only after several weeks that he is found out.

As a matter of fact, they'd really like to have him in the school if only he'd behave decently, for he knows all the work, and goes up from form to form with amazing rapidity, starting with algebra in the bottom form on Monday, and finishing by reading aloud in the top form on Friday afternoon. He yells '1066! 1066!' when he has nothing else to do, and the Doctor, who is rather deaf, likes to hear him.

Then he is very fond of games. His favourite game is cricket, and he's got a special bat. When he plays he presses a button in the handle, and the bat spreads out more than a foot wide. It's quite impossible to get him out.

The Doctor has a megaphone, and when he uses it you can hear him well all over that vast place.

'We will adjourn for games,' he said. 'A match will be played against a team of fully grown dwarfs from Tower 117. They call themselves the Roast Chestnuts.'

Here Noddy Ninety, who had pushed up to the front, said in his piercing voice, 'Put me in last, and all of you get out for ducks.'

Everybody laughed at this, and they adjourned to the green outside, to find that the team of dwarfs had already arrived. They had all been lowered by ropes and pulleys from an immense shelf of building some fifty storeys up.

The Doctor escaped to his study, which is on the first storey and overlooks the pitch. He really hates watching games, but now and then he comes to the window and shouts as if he were interested.

They soon started the match. The Roast Chestnuts went in first, and a fine score they made. They actually made 1,027 before they were out. One dwarf, an excitable little chap called Whiffam, hit a hundred fours without a break.

At last he was caught out by Noddy Ninety, who at that moment was not looking at the game, but was holding out his hands for a meat pie which a dwarf was offering him from a second-storey window. The ball hit a wall, and bounced into his hands, so Whiffam was out.

The Roast Chestnuts were very much elated at the score, and promised each other such treats as boiled jelly-fish, ram-marrow tarts, and a kind of sweet called 'Coggins' to celebrate. Their spirits rose still higher when Dr Lyre's boys had their innings, for they were all coming out for ducks. Whiffam was a good bowler too, and as stump after stump fell he leaped for joy.

At last Ninety went in, carrying his celebrated bat. At first he pretended to play very badly, and nearly came out.

Whiffam gave an elated cry, and sent down a fast one. Ninety hit this very quickly right on to Whiffam's bald head. It glanced off, and he scored two.

Then he began to hit out. He can hit the ball anywhere he likes. He put one ball through Dr Lyre's study window. It came crashing on to his desk and smashed an ink bottle, and the Doctor, though secretly annoyed, went to the window, and shouted, 'Well played!'

When Noddy Ninety was tired of hitting sixes, he began to get under the ball and hit up. He sent a ball up with such force that it hit one of the eagles that was floating about near the top of the towers, and the infuriated bird came down and attacked him.

By this time a tremendous crowd of onlookers had gathered. Thousands of windows had opened, but it was somewhat dangerous to look out of them with Noddy batting.

Finally, when only a six was wanted to win, Noddy Ninety got right underneath a slow ball, and really lifted it into the air. They watched it soar up and up until it became a speck, then it gradually curved over the tower and vanished.

There was a resounding cheer, and even the dwarfs, though malicious in disposition, seemed to be pleased at Ninety's wonderful display.

By this time the sun was setting. It soon gets dark amid those vast mountains of stone, and Uncle's party decided to go home.

They went back a different way.

They took a circular staircase to the seventh storey, where they found a man in an oyster stall who directed them to a long broad passage hung with red cloth. It ran downwards, and in the middle a stream of oil flowed rapidly. I think this stream goes to feed the oil lake below, but it's also a very handy means of transport, for on it are floating some small rafts, and you just get on one of these and float along till you come to the end of the passage. There the oil stream runs to the left, under a low arch, and you get off.

Right in front of them, when they stepped off the raft, was a tube train, and, to their surprise, Noddy Ninety was driving it. Uncle asked him how he had got there so quickly and he told them that they had come a long way round.

If they had simply stepped into the first doorway past the school entrance, they would have found a slanting lift, which would have brought them to the tube in less than three minutes.

They had a pleasant ride back, and Uncle rewarded Noddy Ninety for his superb playing with a basket of buttered biscuits, and ninepence in cash.

7. Rudolph Arrives

IT was Saturday. Uncle was taking up his rent from the dwarfs. When they come to pay him, they have a long ride on the circular railway and through many winding passages.

The hall was full of a pushing, yelling mass of the little men. They were packed in so closely that every now and then the Old Monkey would run rapidly over their heads to see Uncle, and then back again.

When they had paid, they all struggled back through the crowd to the green space in front of Homeward, where they found presents waiting for them. There were two thousand six hundred dwarfs, and piled up on the lawn were two thousand six hundred linen bags, containing raisins, bananas and motoring chocolate.

So, after all, their rent is not excessive, as it includes free electric light and gas for cooking and heating, as well as the presents.

As Uncle was putting the two thousand six hundred farthings into a large bag, the door opened, and Butterskin Mute, the farmer, appeared. He was wearing a smock-frock, and carried a rake. He had brought Uncle a netful of green coconuts, to which he's rather partial, and as he was eating these, Uncle told the Old Monkey to bring Mute a bottle of Sharpener Cordial. Sharpener Cordial is a sort of fizzy drink. You put some pink powder at the bottom of a long glass, then add about a tablespoonful of water; it turns blue and expands till it fills the glass.

Mute put down his glass with a sigh of pleasure.

'I thought I would tell you,' he said then, 'that I passed Badfort this morning, and Beaver Hateman seemed to be ill. There were two fellows winding ropes round his stomach, while he groaned. Then he lay down flat on a big stone that had been warmed in the fire. As I passed, he shook his fist at me, and shouted:

' "Tell Uncle from me I don't mind poisoning people outright, that's all fair and square; but I've never sunk so low as to send anybody a bottle of poison labelled 'Stomach Joy'. Once I get rid of this pain he's for it!" '

Uncle laughed.

'I thought that bottle would ginger him up,' he said cheerfully, 'and I guessed he would drink the lot. I've often heard him say that he swallows a whole bottle of medicine at once ... All the same, I think we had better strengthen our defences a bit, as he'll be in an ugly temper when he recovers.'

Just then the telephone bell rang, and the Old Monkey went to answer it. He soon came back, beaming, and with his eyes sparkling with pleasure.

'It's Mr Rudolph, sir; he told me to tell you that he was getting off at Mother Jones's siding, and that he had his own car in the train, and would ride here.'

'That's good,' said Uncle. 'The Hateman crowd will be watching for him at every station, but they'll never think of Mother Jones's siding!'

As a matter of fact, Mother Jones's siding is on a piece of rusty railway on the other side of the marsh. It's really disused, but you can push a special train along to it very cautiously. Rudolph was actually going to leave the train on the other side of Badfort, and then ride straight to his brother's in a small portable car that he was bringing with him.

It's really amusing. Every time there's trouble with the Badfort lot, he comes to help Uncle, and every time they try to stop him. But he works out a new route to puzzle them. There's no end to his resource.

Soon he arrived. He bumped a bit in his car, as he crossed the bridge.

Rudolph is short and laconic in his talk. He is thinner than Uncle, and quicker. He had brought with him in the car nothing but three large crossbows and a toothbrush.

'You'd better have the car looked at,' he said to the Old Monkey. 'Someone shot an arrow at the back wheel; it only grazed it, but I believe there's a slow puncture. The tyre seems to be going down a bit.'

'Have something to eat,' said Uncle, hospitably.

'Thanks, I'm not hungry. Shot down some breadfruit from a tall tree as I came along. I rushed the car along as it fell, and cooked it on the radiator. It was really excellent, like hot muffin.'

The Old Monkey rubbed his hands. He is well used to Rudolph's promptness and resource, but this was something new, even to him.

'What's that on the table?' said Rudolph. 'Oh, Sharpener Cordial. I'll have a glass, please. Wish I'd had some in the jungle.'

'Did you have a good ride from Mother Jones's?'

'Oh, so so. I got on all right till I got near Badfort. Then I saw a chap watching me, big chap covered with jelly. He seems to live in the pay-box of a disused bathing pool near the marsh. I saw him reach for the telephone, but I put in a quick shot that knocked the instrument to bits.'

Uncle looked at the Old Monkey. This was valuable information. They had often puzzled during the long winter evenings as to where Jellytussle lived.

'By the way,' continued Rudolph, 'they appeared to be holding military exercises in that field at the back of Badfort. They were throwing duck bombs at a big dummy elephant!'

Duck bombs burst when they hit you, and cover you from head to foot with a liquid which looks like lemonade but instantly turns into a tough jelly which is almost impossible to remove; in fact, you can't get it off for hours, and in the meantime you can only move very slowly, as if you were in a gigantic spider's web. You will not be surprised to hear that the Badfort people are always using them.

Uncle snorted, but just then the Old Monkey called out:

'Oh, I say, look here, sir! See what's happening at Badfort.'

The windows were open, and a faint cheer was wafted across. They all got telescopes and field-glasses and looked out. A singular scene met their eyes.

An old man with a short grey beard was arriving at Badfort. He was mounted in a broken cart pulled by the Wooden-Legged Donkey. A piece of one of the wheels was right out, so that it jarred him painfully at each revolution; nevertheless he maintained an upright position, and an appearance of great dignity.

'That's old Nailrod Hateman, Nailrod's father,' said Uncle. 'This is a bigger thing than I thought.'

Obviously the Badfort crowd were immensely cheered by the arrival of old Nailrod. Beaver Hateman seemed somewhat better, though he was still a good deal bent as he stepped forward. Filljug Hateman followed him with a small keg of hot Black Tom. The old man took very little notice of them. He accepted the keg of Black Tom, elevated it, and absently poured the lot down his throat. He was dressed in a sack suit of purple colour. Then he motioned to them to unload the cart. The luggage seemed to consist entirely of pumpkins, but the Old Monkey knew better. They were duck bombs.

Old Nailrod seemed to be addressing them. He kept pointing to Badfort, and frowning, as if remarking on the shabby appearance of the building. Then he contemptuously kicked on one side a little egg bomb, which a young captive badger was filling with glue, ink and tin-tacks. He seemed to be preaching a sort of sermon to them, for they all looked very serious. Then he looked across at Uncle's.

All at once he saw Uncle and instantly took up a telescope to look at him. Uncle was just opening his mouth to laugh, when there was a hissing noise, and a steel dart struck deeply into his trunk.

He gave a loud trumpet of rage and despair, and then began to call in a soft voice for Magic Ointment and Doctor Bunker.

Meanwhile the Badfort crowd cheered loudly. Old Hateman calmly put his telescope away. It was a telescope combined with an air-gun, and you both sighted and fired at the same time. Quite a new weapon, and one that promised to be useful.

The Old Monkey reached for the telephone and called for

LEVENBURY OOOOOOOOO

That's Dr Bunker's number.

They only get Dr Bunker when Uncle believes that he is seriously injured.

While he was coming, the Old Monkey was rubbing Uncle with Magic Ointment, which soon began to cure him; in fact, he was nearly all right when the loud braying of a horn was heard, and Dr Bunker drew up.

He was riding in a flag-decorated lorry with about twenty of his students, and they all kept up a monotonous chorus as they pointed to him:

'He is great! He will cure you!'

Then they lifted from the floor of the lorry framed testimonials and letters of thanks, while one of them displayed a huge card on which was written:

> One hundred thousand people cured
> by Dr Bunker this month!

On the other side of the card was a picture of a hospital empty, and with all the nurses leaving.

The Doctor was a tall fat man with immense moustaches. As soon as he saw Uncle he said:

'This is a serious case!'

As he said this, his twenty assistants all bowed to the ground, and said in a low, monotonous chant:

'A serious case, but he can cure you!'

'Now,' said Dr Bunker at last, 'just blow through your trunk to let me see if that's all right.'

Uncle immediately did so, and blew so hard that the Doctor, who was standing right in front of him, got the full force of the blast and staggered.

He nearly fell over, and Rudolph laughed, but his laughter was drowned in a mighty chorus from the twenty:

'A cure! A perfect cure!'

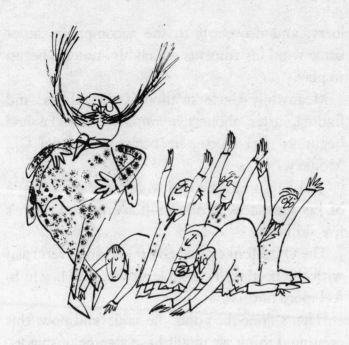

When the Doctor had pulled himself together, he said in rather a surly voice:

'Not much wrong with the trunk, anyhow. How's your head?'

'Rather bad,' said Uncle.

The Doctor pulled out from his pocket a small packet of tablets. 'Headache Mixture!' he said. 'Take three of these after we leave, and five minutes later your head will be as clear as a bell.'

Uncle took the tablets and handed him two pound notes. Dr Bunker bowed his way to the lorry, and drove off to the accompaniment of some wind instruments which his students began to play.

Meanwhile Uncle swallowed the tablets, and finding, after about five minutes, that he had begun to feel worse, he beckoned to the Old Monkey.

'Just run up to the Old Man's and get a bottle of his Headache Producer (for enemies). Here's five shillings.'

The Old Monkey rushed off and soon returned with the bottle. Uncle took a dose, and began to feel more normal.

'That's done me good,' he said, 'and now, this evening, I think we might have a game of spigots. We can't always be watching against enemies, so I vote we have a little fun.'

Uncle likes playing spigots because he always wins. You play it in this way: the Old Monkey puts some wooden boxes at the end of the hall, then you throw balls into them. It's quite an easy game, because the Old Monkey brings all the balls back. Uncle had a match with Rudolph and Cowgill and Butterskin Mute. They played twenty-six games and Uncle won them all. You can't beat Uncle as a thrower. He was quite willing to play even longer, but Rudolph was tired and wanted to turn in.

Cowgill and Mute went on for a bit longer and Uncle rewarded them with good presents. He gave Mute a new lawn-mower, and he gave Cowgill sixty-five pounds of corned beef in five-pound tins.

So they all went cheerfully to bed, the Old Monkey too, for he always gets sevenpence halfpenny for fetching balls.

8. A Quiet Morning

THE next day, they all had a rest in the morning. There was almost complete silence at Badfort. The Badfort gang seemed to be having a late sleep.

'They were up late last night celebrating old Mr Hateman's arrival to help them with preparations,' said the Old Monkey.

'Don't say "old Mr Hateman" in that respectful way. I shall begin to think you are disloyal enough to admire him!'

'Sorry,' replied the Old Monkey. 'I didn't mean to say that!'

A sleepy feeling seemed to be over everyone that day. About eleven o'clock, the inhabitants of Badfort began to build a monster fire in front of the main gateway, tearing down window frames and doors from the upper storeys to do so.

'It's a marvel that there's any of that building left,' said Rudolph. He had come down at last, and had breakfasted, and was now scouring the country with his powerful field-glasses.

'Oh, I expect they are welcoming a few people today,' replied Uncle carelessly.

The fact is that these periodical campaigns against Uncle seem to be the occasion for a good deal of entertaining on both sides. Each party appears to be unable to move until a number of relatives and friends arrive to help.

Uncle had two powerful assistants arriving in the afternoon, and it was pretty evident that the Badfort lot were getting ready for someone to join them. By common consent all parties seemed agreed on a peaceful morning, so they went out on the green outside Homeward and settled down by the side of the moat for a quiet rest. When they were all in deckchairs, with buckets of tea and coffee by their sides and crates of fruit and nuts at their elbows, Rudolph quietly produced a little well-worn volume from his pocket.

'I thought you might like to hear a few extracts from my diary,' he said.

Whenever he comes he reads them some of his diary. He's a wonderful big-game hunter and traveller, but his diary is rather lengthy, and repeats itself a bit. Uncle can't bear it, and always goes to sleep when Rudolph reads it aloud, but the Old Monkey loves it, and so do Butterskin Mute and Whitebeard. But Alonzo S. Whitebeard chiefly loves it because sometimes Rudolph will give a few pennies at the end of a reading; he is so greedy that he often begins to applaud in the wrong place in his eagerness to delight Rudolph.

So they sat there in a semi-circle, the water of the moat shining in the sun, and a beautiful feeling of quiet in the air.

Rudolph began to read.

'I'll start with yesterday's date, and then read backwards,' he said.

'May 11th. Arrived at Homeward. Had an excellent lunch en route of a breadfruit, which I cooked on the radiator of my car. Afterwards my brother was wounded in the trunk by a steel dart, fired with uncommon skill from Badfort...'

'I say,' grumbled Uncle, who wasn't asleep yet, 'I don't like that phrase about "uncommon skill". It sounds as though you admired those hounds.'

'It's all right,' said Rudolph, hastily turning a few pages. 'I'll just read a little further back:

> *'April 2nd. I am now in the celebrated Despair Valley. I have little hope of ever getting out. Over my head tower great cliffs of basalt. My last ration of dried musk-ox flesh is lying at my feet . . .'*

Here Uncle began to snore gently.

> *'Not scores, but hundreds of wolves are moving stealthily up. I string my crossbow. I have just one bolt left –'*

'Good!' said Alonzo S. Whitebeard, who felt that the time had come for him to say something.

Rudolph glanced at him severely.

The Old Monkey's eyes were alive with light, as he gazed in rapturous admiration at the great hunter.

> *'I find that I have one small duck bomb, preserved from a previous visit to Homeward. I hurl the bomb at the leader of the pack. It bursts and*

covers him with a yellow fluid which sends out a very curious smell. He grows suspicious, and raps with his foot on the ground.

'*It is the signal of retreat.*

'*The other wolves slink away. The leader of the pack tries to do so, but the glue-like fluid makes him a prisoner.*

'*Moving away from me are no less than nine hundred wolves. Scanty would have been my chance, if they had come on.*'

The Old Monkey seemed delighted by this narrative. 'Read us some more, sir!' he said eagerly.

'Let me see,' said Rudolph, 'the next few pages are rather ordinary.

'*April 19th. Shot three grizzlies before breakfast.*

'*April 20th. Cross Never-Never Creek which the Indians say is unfordable at this time of the year.*

'Ah, here is something more interesting:

'*April 22nd. An old chief came in tonight to say that the Volcano at Lester-Lester Range would*

shortly be in action. Said he knew this because a
wizard, Snipehazer by name, had told him . . .'

At this point they were interrupted by a sound
of cheering over at Badfort, and, looking through
field-glasses, they were able to see that someone
important was arriving.

Uncle was awake by this time, and looking
through a long telescope he exclaimed:

'I say, I really believe Hootman is coming out to
join them.'

There was no doubt about it, a shadowy figure dressed in a wisp-like sack suit was slowly emerging from a small door at the left-hand side of the fire. It was hard to make him out clearly – he was so vague and misty, but it was Hootman right enough – Hootman, the arch contriver of schemes against Uncle. Hootman really is a sort of ghost, but a very inferior one. The other ghosts, of which there are many living at the Haunted Tower of Uncle's, will have nothing to do with him, and so he came to live at Badfort.

As soon as he appeared Beaver Hateman rushed forward, a plate of hot pork in his hand.

It looked strange to see the spectre holding the plate. Yet it appeared to be making preparations to eat the pork, for with its free arm it drew a sleeve across its shadowy mouth.

Just then Rudolph reached for his crossbow.

'Watch me,' he said. 'I don't think it will be possible to injure that phantom, but I *think* I can knock that plate out of its hand!'

There was a sharp twang, and a moment later the plate vanished.

Hootman threw up his arms, and gave a fine exhibition of rage. It looked very strange to see his ghostly indignation. Rudolph burst out laughing, and reached for his diary.

'I think,' he said, 'that today's entry will be unique in a small way!'

He began to write:

May 11th. Anger of a ghost: I have shot so many things that I began to think that there was nothing else for me to shoot, but today I think I even frightened a ghost . . .

9. At Dearman's Store

TWO people were knocking at the moat gate. Uncle was glad to see them, for they were two specially useful fellows, Cloutman and Gubbins.

They often come over to stay for a time. Gubbins is a wonderfully strong man. He always arrives with a very heavy trunk and the first thing he does is to rush up the big staircase, carrying his trunk balanced on one hand. Everyone likes to see him do it.

Cloutman, on the other hand, cannot carry great weights, but he can strike terrible blows. One smack with his fist can make a lion stagger and fall. He has large bony hands. Uncle was very glad to see these two, as they are specially useful for subduing the Badfort crowd.

Just as he was welcoming them, a nasty laugh was heard in the distance, and Alonzo S. Whitebeard was observed to turn pale.

'I believe that's your stepfather, Whitebeard,' said Uncle.

Whitebeard looked depressed, but reluctantly admitted that it was so.

He was coming along now, singing as he walked. His voice seems to have some kind of sickening effect, for the moment you hear it you feel rather ill, or at any rate seedy and depressed. He arrived at the gate, and then said with a ghastly smile:

'I've come to offer my services to you, sir, knowing that you may be attacked.'

He made a silly preposterous bow as he said these words, and gave vent to a guffaw so abominable that a large glass jug on the table cracked from top to bottom.

Before Uncle could reply, Cloutman said:

'Excuse me, sir, but as we were coming along, I heard that old man offer his services to Beaver Hateman.'

'Ha! Ha!' said old Whitebeard, with an atrocious chuckle that made everyone shudder. 'That's a good joke, the best I've ever heard.'

'Be silent,' said Uncle, 'and remove yourself or you will be kicked up!'

This threat had its effect, and the old man swaggered off with a scream of foul merriment that sickened all listeners.

The fact is that old Whitebeard is detested by everybody. The Badfort lot won't have him at any price; neither will Uncle.

After this unsavoury interlude, and as the Badfort people appeared to have settled down for an afternoon of planning, Uncle thought they might safely go out for a bit. A visit on the traction engine to a shop kept by Duncan Dearman in Badgertown would be a change.

Accordingly, they collected together a strong company on the engine and tender: Rudolph, the Old Monkey, Cloutman, Gubbins and Alonzo S. Whitebeard.

There was a certain amount of hissing and screaming from Badfort as they started, and a few arrows were shot, but there seemed to be a general agreement to leave each other alone for a while. The fact is that old Whitebeard has such a noxious influence that for some hours after he has been about, Uncle and the Badfort people feel fairly friendly towards each other.

So they went on merrily to Badgertown.

Duncan Dearman has a little shop in a side street just opposite Cheapman's huge store. All his goods are frightfully dear, so you can guess that he does very little business; in fact the only customer he has is Uncle, and if Uncle was not sometimes rather fond of showing off he would not go there either.

When they arrived at Dearman's, he was just changing a ticket on a thin, battered, tin milk jug. The ticket said:

YESTERDAY'S PRICE   £21
TODAY'S PRICE   £25

As he adjusted the ticket he wept loudly, and bemoaned his lack of customers.

Just then he caught sight of Uncle, and came running out with his face all smiles. He rushed up to him, and began to lead him into the shop.

'Come in, sir, come in at once!'

Uncle could hardly get into the shop, but there was a great armchair there into which he managed to wedge himself. When he was in it, the place was about full, and little Dearman had to climb about as best he could, crawling along the shelves, and standing on the counter. The others stayed outside and looked through the window, and they were joined by a lot of other folk from Badgertown, for a visit from Uncle was always a great event!

'Can I show you a nice clock, sir?' said Dearman, in an ingratiating manner, displaying as he spoke an alarm clock with one leg off, priced £30 7s. 4d.

Uncle didn't want the clock, so he showed him a shabby moth-eaten overcoat marked £21 10s. od. This was too small, so Uncle refused it.

There was little else in the shop, but after a long search he found an artificial pineapple, labelled

'For the Fruit Stand' and priced £33 7s. od., and Uncle bought it at once.

Uncle is the last person in the world to put artificial fruit on his sideboard, but he can't resist anything that is capable of being thrown. He took out his money-bag, and paid at once in new pound notes and clean silver.

He wouldn't buy anything else, so he drank a mug of coffee that Dearman brought him, and then picked up the artificial pineapple, and heaved himself out of the armchair.

As he reached the door, he heard laughter. Then, looking down the street, he saw a sight that filled him with fury.

Beaver and old Nailrod Hateman had followed him to the shop and they were actually giving a comic imitation in the street of the scene that had just taken place.

Old Nailrod Hateman had bought a halfpenny armchair from Cheapman's, and was sitting in it, while Beaver Hateman presented to him a number of articles: a broken spade handle marked £187 4s. 3d., a saucepan marked £88 5s. 7d. and an empty cocoa tin marked £25. As he offered these things, Nailrod Hateman kept saying in a loud imperious voice:

'No, that won't do; show me something else!'

They also had Filljug Hateman disguised as Whitebeard, pretending to weep and saying, 'Oh, sir, you'll ruin yourself.'

Large numbers of badgers were standing round, nearly splitting their little hides with laughter.

Even as Uncle looked, Nailrod Hateman extended his hand and took up a broken mousetrap with an enormous red ticket on which was written: 'Only £500 4s. 2½d. today, £21 9s. 0d. yesterday.

He said in a languid voice:

'I'll take that.'

When Uncle saw this insulting mockery he turned scarlet, and, without waiting a moment, flung the pineapple right at Nailrod Hateman. It knocked him completely out of his chair. Beaver Hateman seemed to be too astonished to reply, so Uncle strolled haughtily by, and they all climbed into the traction engine and drove off.

Uncle got home in good spirits. He had lost his pineapple but he was very delighted to have had a return blow at Nailrod Hateman. The steel dart injury of the day before was now avenged.

When they got back to Homeward there was good news. The Marquis of Wolftown had heard that Uncle was likely to be besieged, and had sent him as a present two hundred cart-loads of honey and strawberry jam, and six thousand cases of condensed milk.

This was delightful, and Uncle's high spirits were further increased by an incident which occurred while they were having tea by the moat. Beaver Hateman appeared at the drawbridge carrying with him a white flour bag, which was supposed to be a white flag.

'Flag of truce, young man,' he said to the Old Monkey. 'Tell Uncle that I want to go up to the Old Man's for medicine. Mr Nailrod Hateman's got a very bad headache.'

Uncle said he could go, if Cloutman and Gubbins walked on each side of him.

All the way through the hall Beaver Hateman kept muttering, 'Yes, this place is all right. Look at that golden jug, and those tapestries, and all that silver plate! We'll know what to do with it when this place belongs to us.'

He was soon escorted out of the hall, but as he left he turned to Uncle.

'Yes,' he said, 'it's all right knocking old men about with artificial fruit, and receiving cart-loads of honey and stuff the same afternoon;

you've had a full day, I grant you. But there's tomorrow, and the day after, and the next day. Perhaps something's going to happen that will surprise you a little.'

10. They Visit Watercress Tower

IT was a few days after, and Uncle was about to have his music lesson. He has a great fondness for music, but is rather a poor player. He is trying to learn the bass viol, and there's a little man called Gordono who comes to teach him. His real name is Thomaso Elsicar Gordono. He's an Italian, and everyone calls him the Maestro. The worst of it is he has such a dreadful temper. He gets into a passion over his music, and tries to throw himself out of the window because he can't bear to hear things played badly. He is always accompanied by a small lion, called the Little Lion. No one knows his real name.

That afternoon, the Maestro came as usual, and walking with him was his pet. Although he's grown up, the lion is hardly larger than an Airedale dog, but he's fearfully tough and compact. He also has one curious power. He can make himself heavy beyond all reason. He does it in a moment. Try to get him out of a room. You might think it would be easy enough, but the moment you try to move him you find your mistake. He doesn't resist you. He simply makes himself *heavy*, and though you'd hardly believe it, he must weigh about a ton! He seems to like music for he listens attentively to the Maestro.

That afternoon the Maestro played a brilliant waltz of his own composition on the piano, and then started to teach Uncle. Uncle is a bit heavy

with the bow, and made one or two false notes. The moment he did so, the Maestro threw himself on the ground in a passion, grinding his teeth.

He got up and rushed to the window but realized then that he was on the ground floor. He looked rather sheepish, but contented himself with screaming a little. After a while he cooled down and the lesson proceeded.

When it was over, he said to Uncle:

'Have you ever been to Watercress Tower, where the Little Lion and I live?'

'No,' replied Uncle.

'There you are! There you are!' said the Maestro. 'Yet you can go over and over again to visit Butter-skin Mute's wretched little farm! It's not fair!'

The Little Lion was squatting on a strong thick-legged stool. As the Maestro said these words, he made himself heavy, and the stool immediately collapsed.

'Now,' said Uncle, 'look what you've done! Spoilt a good stool!'

He knew the hopelessness of dragging or kicking the Little Lion out, so he said no more, but turned to the Maestro.

'It's true I've never been to Watercress Tower, but I'll come this afternoon, and – wait a bit – that's Butterskin Mute coming over the drawbridge. I'll bring Mute with me, and the Old Monkey.'

'Righto!' said the Maestro with a smile. He was in high spirits all at once. One good thing about the Maestro is that his rages never last long, or else he would simply wear himself out. He was delighted at the thought of taking Uncle to see his dwelling place. The Little Lion stopped being heavy. He got on to his hind legs and briskly rubbed his eyes, as if preparing them for a good sight.

They set out almost at once. Mute was quite willing to go, for watercress is the one thing he cannot grow, and he had often wondered where Uncle obtained his splendid supplies. He emptied his sack of choice young cabbages on the table, and said that he would like to go immensely.

'You'll want bathing costumes,' said the Maestro. 'I always bring one in my bag and change on the way.'

So they all took bathing costumes. The Maestro said that there was a good place at the foot of the tower where they could change.

'Shall we have to take any provisions?' said Uncle.

'Oh no,' replied the Maestro carelessly, 'there's always a bit going up there.'

So they set out. They went to the end of the hall and took a tube labelled Biscuit Tower. When they got to the Biscuit Tower they found a junction, and another tube labelled Watercress Tower. They were glad to find that it was driven by Noddy Ninety. They went through a lot of tunnels.

At last they reached the base of Watercress Tower. It was a very wet place, and they could easily see the need for bathing suits. Right up the side of the tower was a gigantic salmon ladder. I don't know whether you have seen a salmon ladder in a stream, but they are like steps with water running over them. They all changed into their bathing costumes (except the Little Lion, who travels in his own coat all the time), and started up the ladder.

It was an exhausting business after the first two hundred feet, and Uncle stopped a minute and said to the Maestro:

'Do you come up and down this every time you want to go out?'

'Every time,' replied the Maestro firmly. 'There is an electric lift in the tower, but I can't stick the things. They make me feel wobbly inside and the Little Lion hates them so much that when he gets on, he makes himself heavy, and then the lift won't work.'

'Well, I suppose there's nothing for it but to go on,' said Uncle gloomily. 'I suppose now you're going to tell me the usual tale about it being only twenty storeys higher up!'

The Maestro was so enraged at this speech that he threw himself right off the salmon ladder. However, he missed the rocks, and, after swimming about for a bit, grew cooler and began to climb after them.

'I vote we sit down,' said Uncle, panting. 'There's a pool here where we can sit down while the Maestro catches us up!'

It felt very nice there with the water rushing past. The walls of all the towers looked pretty too, for they had ferns growing on them.

They all felt rested when the Maestro arrived. He seemed to be in the best of tempers again, and had quite forgotten his annoyance. At last they reached the top. They arrived at a place where water came cascading out of a huge open door, and when they got inside they found themselves in a large room, with a stream running along the floor. They went through this and found themselves in another room about two feet deep in water, with stainless steel tables, chairs, bookcases, etc.

'I sometimes study here on a hot day,' said the Maestro.

At the end of this room were two doors, with electric bells, and cards pinned beneath them.

One card said:

Mr T. E. Gordono

and the other:

Mr L. Lion

From underneath the doors came the stream of water.

The Maestro now drew out a latchkey and opened the door on the right. It opened on to a waterfall, or rather a flight of steps with water running down them. They waded up these steps, which looked very lovely with the foaming water pouring down them, and with lilies and ferns

growing in the cracks of the stones. Then they found themselves on the shore of a gigantic lake on the top of a tower so huge that it seemed like a mountain. Most of the lake appeared to be overgrown with watercress.

On each side of the waterfall stood a little hut. On the door of one hut was

T. E. GORDONO

and on the other

L. LION

The lake looked fine, for there were cranes and herons flying around and enormous lemon-coloured fish swam lazily by.

The Maestro led them into his hut.

There was very little inside, except a grand piano, a violin and a camp bed. It was hard to see into the Little Lion's hut, for he dived in very quickly to have a rub down, and shut the door after him, but Uncle has very sharp eyes, and he noticed what looked very like a bottle of medicine on the table inside.

The Little Lion soon came out and joined them.

'Well,' said Uncle, 'you've got a snug place up here.'

'Oh, it's all right,' replied the Maestro. 'But the rent's excessive!'

'The rent!' said Uncle severely. 'I don't remember getting any rent from you.'

'I don't pay *you*,' said the Maestro.

'Indeed, and whom do you pay?'

'I always pay a man called Beaver Hateman. When I was looking for rooms in this neighbourhood, he met me, and said that he owned the tower, and that the lion and I could have rooms cheap.'

When Uncle heard this, he trumpeted with rage. 'Beaver Hateman!' he shouted. 'Am I never to get out of sight and hearing of that chap? Here I am on the top of a lonely tower, preparing for a little intellectual conversation, and his hideous trail is here!

'Listen,' he continued, 'the man who charges you rent for these rooms is not only defrauding you, but his very presence is a menace. May I ask you what he charges?'

'He wanted fifty pounds, but I beat him down to twopence.'

'Well, let me tell you that even at twopence per

week you've been done. I only charge a halfpenny per week for large roomy flats, with electric light, and all conveniences.'

When the Maestro heard this, he immediately rushed to the edge of the tower, but the Little Lion followed him, and, seeing that it would be a fatal drop, fixed his teeth in his trousers, made himself heavy and sat down.

The Maestro gave one pull, then, seeing the hopelessness of making a struggle, came quietly back to Uncle.

'I suppose you pay him regularly?' said Uncle.

'Yes, I pay him every quarter; that's two and twopence per quarter. I make him give me a receipt.'

'I should like to see one of these receipts.'

The Maestro reached up to a file, and took down a greasy piece of paper.

Uncle looked at it. It read:

```
to Bever hateman, Esq.,
rent of Rooms on watercress Tower
13 weaks @ 2d.          5/6d
                         2/2

Recieved without thanks
B Hatman
```

'So he tried to make out that thirteen weeks at twopence came to five and sixpence. The scoundrel!'

'Yes, he said he wasn't any good at figures.'

Uncle turned over the receipt. It was written on the back of an old bill which read:

> To Thomas Minifer, Stationer.
>   Supplying 50 black books,
> with 'hating book' inscribed on back
>   50 @ 5/– . . . . £12 10s. 0d.

On the bottom was a note:

> As this account has been presented in various ways during the past five years, we should now like to press for an immediate payment.

Uncle trumpeted again.

'This is vile!' he said. 'He makes out his bill to you on the back of an unpaid bill of his own. I see he signed the receipt in red ink.'

'No, he signed it in his own blood; he just stuck the pen deep in his arm and wrote.'

'His own blood! Is there any end to the man's detestable ways!' Uncle snorted, then went on:

'But wait a bit, you've been supplying me with cress week by week, for which I paid you the very substantial sum of twopence per week.'

'Yes, I used that to pay the rent.'

'So the money I paid for cress went into Hateman's pocket! It's a wonder I haven't been poisoned. Well, in future, you pay me. D'you understand?'

'Certainly. I shall be glad to do so.'

Uncle sat down fuming, but the Maestro brought him some very good cress sandwiches, and, after devouring a few platefuls of these, he felt better. The sun was setting and the great lake was all golden, except for the patches of bright-green cress.

A gentle breeze blew, and the Maestro went to the piano and began to play. You'd be surprised to hear how well the music sounded up there. The Little Lion seemed to be carried away by it, for he sat perfectly still, except for a flickering half-smile, and the rhythmic wagging of his tail. The Old Monkey and Butterskin Mute were enraptured.

Uncle began to feel calm and happy.

'After all,' he said to himself, 'I have not come here in vain. I have exposed and removed a grievous wrong; the afternoon has been by no means wasted.'

Before he left, he bestowed on the Maestro the sum of five shillings to repay him for some of the wrongly charged rent, and he gave the Little Lion a voucher for the same amount to spend at the Old Man's on medicine. That little creature is mad on physic and drugs (which he certainly does not need), for he snatched the voucher from Uncle as though he were gaining a fortune.

Uncle soon bade them farewell. They went down by the first lift they saw. It stopped for a moment at the bottom of the salmon ladder, where they collected their clothes, then took them most of the way back to Homeward.

Uncle was curious to see how the Little Lion spent his money, so, after tea, he slipped up the elevator to the tower where the Old Man has his medicine store.

He crept up and peeped through the window.

Yes, there was the Little Lion. He had already purchased a bottle of Headache Mixture, and one of Headache Producer (for enemies), besides two bottles of Rheumatism Mixture, and a flask of Stomach Joy.

Uncle smiled, and forbore to warn him, as he thought a sharp lesson might do the stubborn little creature good.

But the lion must have an inside of brass, for Uncle heard afterwards from the Maestro that he drank the whole flask of Stomach Joy and liked it, and seemed to be exceptionally bright and active next day.

11. A Visit to Owl Springs

IT was Uncle's birthday, and he had planned a celebration. He told the Old Monkey at breakfast that they were going to Owl Springs. The Old Monkey jumped for joy. If there is any treat that he likes, it is this visit. The springs are not up to much, and it's very hard to get a good look at the owl, but all the same there's something fascinating about the place.

People come from all round, especially when there is a rumour that the owl is about, but, as a matter of fact, the only person so far who had really seen the owl was the Old Monkey. One wet Friday night when everyone else had gone away he saw it quite clearly for about five minutes. Most people have not even had a glimpse of it, and those who have are notable characters for the rest of their lives.

They telephoned to Cowgill for the traction engine. Although it was Uncle's birthday, he had only received a few presents as yet, a packet of ginger-nuts from the Old Monkey, and some mangoes from Butterskin Mute, while Alonzo S. Whitebeard had simply given him a medal that he had picked up in the street. He gave it to Uncle because he thought it was no good, but he was surprised to discover later that it had a very useful quality that nobody had expected. Uncle found this out by accident, while they were waiting for the traction engine. It suddenly turned blue when he stepped on to a little mound of earth, then became silver-coloured again when he stepped off it. He had the curiosity to dig the mound away a little, and found, just under the surface, nine half-crowns wrapped in grease-proof paper. It was evidently a buried-treasure detector. Uncle was delighted, for he had often wanted a thing of this kind, but Whitebeard was very depressed, and wished heartily that he had been generous enough to buy Uncle the halfpenny typewriter that he had been looking at for days in Cheapman's window.

At last they started, Uncle, the Old Monkey and Alonzo S. Whitebeard, with Cowgill as driver and engineer.

The road to Owl Springs goes through a deep valley. Lots of people were also travelling there that day, some on foot, some by car, but most by motor coach. A man called Onion Sam gets up these trips during the May to September season.

They chug-chugged along steadily. As they approached a place where the road was up, they heard the noise of hooves, and Beaver Hateman galloped up to them on his Wooden-Legged Donkey. He was followed by Nailrod Hateman on his lean goat, Toothie.

'Hallo, Uncle!' said Beaver Hateman. 'Going to see the owl?'

'I hope to do so,' replied Uncle calmly.

'Well, I don't think you will; I passed Wizard Blenkinsop on the road, and he assured me that the owl would not be seen after ten this morning. It's now half past nine and we shall be there in ten minutes, while you'll get there about eleven! So long, Uncle!'

He galloped off like the wind.

Uncle was rather irritated at this speech, but cheered himself up with a second breakfast of coconuts and chocolate ice-cream from an electroplated bucket.

Beaver Hateman was right. It was nearly eleven when they reached the famous Owl Springs. The narrow valley was packed with people, who were walking round, dropping litter and looking at the springs. These springs are disappointing at the first glance, a mere muddy trickle of water coming down between bushes, but they are fascinating all the same, and it seems well worthwhile going there even if you don't see the owl.

Halfway up the valley is a large enclosure labelled *Trade Exhibition*. Uncle was in no hurry, and seeing that there was such a crowd, he thought he might as well visit this first. They went in, paying a halfpenny for the whole party at the

turnstile. It was quite a good exhibition with a large number of stalls.

One was kept by a dull, heavy ox. He appeared to have only one thing on his stall, a box, pink in colour, called BIRTHDAY BOX.

Uncle asked the price.

'A thousand pounds,' replied the ox in a slow, dull voice, 'and I won't come down a farthing in my price.'

There was something about this box that took Uncle's fancy, and though he thought the price high he paid it in clean hundred-pound notes. The moment he did so, the ox took from behind the counter a little board marked STALL CLOSED and prepared to leave.

'Can you tell me the way to Cheapman's store?' he asked the Old Monkey. 'I've heard that you can get lashings of hay there for a bob.'

The Old Monkey directed him, and smiled as he did so. A shilling spent at Cheapman's on hay would provide any ox with a larger pile than he could possibly devour during the rest of his life.

There were a lot of other stalls, but Uncle was rather interested in a small quiet shop with a sign which read:

> **THE BOOKMAN**
> Bookseller and Stationer

It seemed quite an ordinary sign, but The Bookman was the actual name of the shopkeeper. He was the son of a famous boxer called Wallaby Bookman, who had married a young woman with the curious name of Mable The. He had naturally gone into the book trade on growing up.

The Bookman was sitting on a bench outside his shop reading a small book, and every now and then he marked some places in it with a carpenter's pencil. When Uncle asked to see his shop he simply pointed into the doorway with his thumb.

They went in. The shop consisted of a single room built of thick square logs. On one side of it was a shelf with about twenty books. They were all the same, *The History of Owl Springs*.

'We've got this,' said Uncle. 'Let's get on to the springs.'

He walked out.

On their way Nailrod Hateman passed them.

'It's all over for the day,' he said. 'Oh, what a time we've had! I saw the owl myself – looked straight at it for more than an hour!'

This was most likely a lie, and they pretended not to hear. A gleam of sun came out, and everything looked rather pretty, in spite of the mass of litter left by the excursionists. Just as they were looking at the thin trickle of muddy water, a wonderful thing happened.

From behind a low bush on the left, *the owl appeared*! He flew straight to a withered twig, and sat there looking at them.

Uncle reached for his cine-camera, and took some shots of the owl from different positions.

He did not venture to speak for fear that the owl should go.

For twenty minutes the owl stayed, minutes filled with rapture. Then it gave a low hoot, preened its feathers, and slowly flew off.

They all kept silent for a time. Uncle's face was glowing, and as for the Old Monkey, he swung himself up to the branch of a nearby tree and hung there by his hands and feet.

At last they spoke:

'Congratulations, sir,' said the Old Monkey. 'I always wanted you to see it, and I was always sorry that you weren't there when I had that good look, three years ago.'

Uncle said nothing for a long time. He was so full of solemn joy. At last he drew a deep breath.

'Gratification,' he said, 'is a poor word to express my feelings at this moment. I am afloat on a sea of foaming joy and delight! For the time being, I will say little, but on many a long winter evening I shall expound to you with suitable words my feelings at this extraordinary event!'

'And I shall love to hear you,' said the Old Monkey simply.

'In the meantime, leave me alone,' said Uncle. 'I want to travel back quietly, reflecting deeply on this glorious hour, and fixing its details in my memory.'

12. The Birthday Evening

AFTER a special birthday banquet that evening Uncle started to open his presents. It was impossible to examine them all at once, so, as it was chilly, Uncle directed his helpers to pile them up in a sort of semi-circular wall round the fireplace.

The fireplace is just like a little house; it has thick walls on three sides, and a little window at the back, looking out on to the moat. There was still room in this monster fireplace for a big table; Uncle's festival chair made of brass, with red velvet cushions; chairs for the rest of them; and also a great cauldron of hot ginger wine, which slowly warmed at the log fire.

'This is very pleasant,' said Uncle. 'And now I think we might have a look at the thousand-pound box I bought today.'

They all gathered round the table, while Uncle examined the box. It was a queer box made of iron and wood with silver nails. It looked pinkish at first, then seemed to turn blue.

He tore off a piece of stiff parchment which was fastened over a hole in the lid, and found an end of touchpaper. There was a note which read:

Light this when the box is in the middle of the table, then look out for a big surprise.

He lit it.

At first it smouldered, then it began to burn with a small green flame, but very clear, and sharp as a sword. It trembled into purple, then pink, then started to fizz and to let out stars. You have seen those fireworks that come out like snakes – well, it was like that on a big scale. A great brown serpent came wobbling and gliding out of the box, and gradually spread its length over the table. It slowly turned a bright gold colour, gave one pop, and from its body came out hundreds of little balloons, blue, red, pink and green. These rapidly swelled out till they were about a foot broad, and floated about the room. It was pretty to see them.

There seemed to be nothing left of the snake, but instead a parcel lay on the table. Uncle began to open it.

It contained a pair of elephant's tusk-tips, cut out of diamonds big enough for a royal crown. Uncle stuck them on the ends of his tusks, and they shone in the firelight splendidly.

When Uncle had admired them for a time he said in an impressive voice:

'I might well have hesitated to spend a thousand pounds on this parcel. Instead of that, I said to myself, "This is your birthday. Gratify that struggling ox!" What is the result? I have gratified myself and him, and we are both happy.'

They were all impressed by this speech, especially Whitebeard, who seemed dazzled.

As the Old Monkey handed round glasses of the hot ginger wine, Uncle went on in a low, dreamy voice:

'That has always been my guiding principle. I was born in the jungle. My parents were poor. A young, tender elephant, I was thrust out into the world at an early age to make a living. My sole starting capital was a halfpenny, but I have built up my fortune on this principle – to do the other person and myself good at the same time.'

Here Uncle drew out a handkerchief, and wiped away a little moisture from his eyes. He gets a lot of pleasure out of feeling sorry for himself when he recollects his early days.

'Nobody present,' he said, 'can remember the bitterness of my early struggles. Even the Old Monkey . . .'

There was a loud scuffling and shrieking in the chimney. Then, with an appalling yell, a dwarfish little man was hurled right down the chimney into the cauldron of hot ginger wine. He made an awful splash, then floundered helplessly in the vat.

Uncle pulled him out, and set him by the fire to dry.

One look was enough to show them who it was. It was Hitmouse, and as Uncle looked up the chimney he saw glaring down on him the degraded face of Beaver Hateman.

'Ha, ha! Uncle,' shouted Hateman. 'I stuck it until you started talking about the Old Monkey, then I threw Hitmouse down to give you a fright; I also want to remind you that when you were talking about yourself you didn't mention the fact that you once STOLE A BIKE!'

When Uncle heard this he was so tremendously enraged that he filled his trunk full of the ginger wine, although it was so hot that it hurt him, and squirted it up the chimney at Hateman.

It struck him with such force that he toppled backwards and fell into the moat with a splash.

Feeling better, Uncle continued with his life story.

'When I had the Old Monkey, I prospered still more. It was then that I took over this castle from Wizard Blenkinsop. Everything would be perfect if it weren't for certain people who live in Badfort —'

As he said this, Beaver Hateman appeared at the little window and began to shout in a loud voice at the window:

'Ha, ha! HE STOLE A BIKE!!'

This was more than Uncle could bear. He rushed to the door. When he came back Hitmouse had disappeared. He had, so the Old Monkey said, slipped up the chimney again.

Uncle said sternly:

'Let us forget this disgraceful episode. And now, before we turn in, we will have a few games.'

They had quite a number, including 'Whitebeard's Buff'. Uncle ties Whitebeard's whiskers round his head, and then Whitebeard has to find the rest of them. He looks funny – a tremendous mop of hair charging round the room. Uncle can play at it splendidly, because he puts out the tip of his trunk, and Whitebeard thinks that he has caught him while he's really quite a long way off.

After a lot of other games, they had light refreshments and then went to bed. In spite of the unpleasant incident at the fire, Uncle felt that he had had a really good birthday.

13. Christmas Eve at Uncle's

IT was now getting well into December, and the weather made it necessary for there to be a kind of truce between Uncle and the people at Badfort. The weather is always positively terrific in December, with deep snow, bitter frosts and lots of blizzards. No one can equal Uncle at snowballing. He has always been the best thrower for miles around, and the way he can whizz a snowball through the air is really unique. Also, he draws fine snow up his trunk, and squirts it out with great force, pushing enemies over backwards into drifts.

There's a long-standing custom, too, that Hateman and his tribe should be invited to Homeward for the Christmas festivities, or at any rate for part of them. Uncle is always saying he is going to give this up, and the Badfort people are always saying they'll never come again, but somehow they turn up.

It was Christmas Eve, and one of the worst winter nights ever known. Snow lay deep on the drawbridge and the frozen moat, but a cheerful company was assembled in Homeward.

Uncle had got off the last of his Christmas presents. For weeks motor lorries had been going out loaded to the roof with cakes, bread, hams, biscuits, chocolate and so on. During the few days before Christmas a gigantic presentation had been made to the dwarfs and other eager neighbours in the towers. At last they were all satisfied. The last Christmas card had been sent off, and all Uncle's guests had arrived except the Badfort crowd.

They were a gay party. Rudolph was there, the Old Monkey, of course, with his father and uncle, besides Mig, Cloutman, Gubbins, Whitebeard, Auntie and the Companion, Noddy Ninety and Don Guzman. Also the One-Armed Badger who had been really happy for the last few weeks, loading himself to the ground with bales of provisions.

Homeward was so resplendent with firelight that they hardly needed the electric lamps.

Then they saw dark figures approaching over the snow, singing as they came. It was the Badfort crowd, and the song they were singing was, as usual, something degraded, and like most of their songs, didn't quite rhyme, but, in compliment to the season, they were not singing anything insulting to Uncle.

> '*Hungry for sausage and* MASH,
> *Or a newspaper full of fried* SCOB,
> *I went to the Palais de* FISH
> *And looked round for something to* GRAB.'

In front of the procession marched Beaver Hateman, carrying on the end of a pole a small tub filled with scob oil, which, I might explain, is made from the scob fish that they catch in the marsh. It burns a very dark red, and sparkles with a bright blue light.

When they got to the door, they piled up their bows and arrows on the threshold, besides some duck bombs they happened to have with them, and walked in unarmed.

They were wearing their usual sack suits, but they had tried their best to make them look festive, by tying on to them sprigs of holly.

They glanced hungrily at the table as they walked in.

Beaver Hateman was the first to approach Uncle.

'Good evening, Uncle,' he said, extending a hand blue with cold, and with a spiky sprig of holly tucked away in the palm.

Uncle did not take his hand, but stood looking coldly at him.

'So you won't shake hands?' began Hateman. 'I think we'd better go back for our duck bombs!'

'I do *not* refuse to shake hands,' Uncle replied, 'but standing at my side is my Aunt, Miss Maidy, and I want to remind you that it is always the custom to shake hands with a lady first.'

'Oh, all right,' said Hateman. Tucking the piece of holly up his sleeve, he shook hands with Auntie and afterwards with Uncle.

The rest were soon introduced. Even Hootman had come, for, being a ghost, he was quite at home on Christmas Eve; Jellytussle was also there, though he had to stand away from the fire, or his jelly would have melted.

It is not the slightest use getting the tribe to sit down at table. Uncle has tried it again and again, but they only smash everything. So they all sit on the hearth round the fire to eat, except Jellytussle, who slowly gnaws a joint of pork on the cool side of the room, and Hootman, who eats his provisions in a gloomy alcove.

They had a mighty feast. Uncle's table was so loaded with provisions that it had actually to be supported in places by casks of ham.

It seemed as though they would never finish, but at last the tables were cleared and they sat down for a time before having games.

There's one item that they always have at Christmas time, and that's an action song version of 'Good King Wenceslas'.

Uncle goes to the window and looks out, while everyone sings the carol, and then Whitebeard comes slowly up, gathering winter fuel, which he does to the manner born, for he has spent his whole life in gathering something or other.

Uncle went to the window. He had clothed himself in a red-and-gold dressing-gown, and looked every inch a king. He held a gilded marlinspike in his hand as a sceptre.

They all began to sing the carol.

Soon Whitebeard came into sight, bent nearly double as he searched for fuel. He was playing his part splendidly and everyone was pleased, when, all at once, a hideous laugh was heard, and White-beard's stepfather appeared on the drawbridge. The moment they saw him, all their spirits fell. He stepped right in front of his son, and looked at Uncle with an odious expression.

'Ha, ha, sir, you're doing "Wenceslas", are you? Well, I'd better be the old man. My stepson won't do; he's too young. I can beat him at gathering fuel, and I can certainly beat him at the flesh-and-wine stunt!'

This was absolutely true.

As he said these words, Beaver Hateman stepped up to Uncle.

'If you admit Whitebeard's stepfather,' he said, 'we're all going home, and that's the truth!'

'Be silent!' said Uncle sternly. Turning to Whitebeard Senior he said in a cold, terrible voice:

'Be gone!'

'Ha, ha! The great Uncle turns away a feeble old man on Christmas Eve!'

His laughter was so atrocious that even Beaver Hateman began to feel ill.

Uncle continued to address old Whitebeard in tones of ice.

'No man, whoever he is, shall be turned empty from my door on Christmas Eve. Take that bag!'

He pointed to a large sack of cakes, sweets and nuts. 'And now, remove yourself, or, even though it's Christmas Eve, I shall have to adopt an extreme course.'

They opened the door wider, and Uncle went back for a run.

Old Whitebeard did not wait.

After this, they soon finished off the action song 'Wenceslas', though the interest in it was not as great as it had been.

When they had finished this, old Nailrod Hateman gave his conjuring display. It was very good, but a bit monotonous. It was called 'The disappearing pork pie'. Uncle put a pork pie on an empty table, and old Nailrod covered it with a handkerchief. When he took it off, the pie was gone. What he really did was to swallow the pie very quickly while he was flicking the cloth off. He did it with such immense speed that you couldn't see it go, only, if you looked very closely, you could see the bulge in his throat as he swallowed it.

He was quite ready to go on with this for a long time, but they soon got tired of his display, and played 'Whitebeard's Buff'.

After that Noddy Ninety gave his action song called 'At the Gates of Metz'. Ninety says that he was educated in Germany, at Metz. Nobody is old enough to contradict him.

He chanted the song in his piercing voice, emphasizing certain words:

> '*On a bitter winter's night*
> *By the gates of* METZ,
> *I waited in the fading light,*
> *In my thin torn* VEST.
>
> '*Only just across the way,*
> *Was a sausage* SHOP;
> *But it was no good to me,*
> *Pfennigs I had* NOT.'

There were a lot of verses to this song and when he had finished, nothing would satisfy him but to start all over again, this time with the verse:

> '*On a bitter winter's night*
> *By the gates of* ULM,
> *I waited in the fading light*
> *With my fingers* NUMB.'

Auntie and Rudolph cut in with an argument as to whether 'Metz' and 'vest' and 'Ulm' and

'numb' were rhymes. Noddy Ninety said, 'We do modern poetry at Dr Lyre's School.'

'Let's have supper,' said Beaver Hateman. 'We've had enough poetry for one evening.'

After supper Uncle said:

'As a great treat tonight, I'm going to let you sleep in the Haunted Tower. I may tell you,' he continued, 'that everyone avoids that place; the last man who tried to sleep there came out in half an hour, unable to speak, and with his hair perfectly white.'

Uncle couldn't have suggested anything better. It's a frightful business getting the Badfort crowd to go to bed, but the moment they heard of the Haunted Tower they were all eager to go.

'Good egg, Uncle!' said Nailrod Hateman. 'I'm surprised at you thinking of anything so sensible: just the binge for Christmas Eve!'

Uncle was glad for them to go. He had stockings to fill, and other things to do, and so he was glad of this quiet hour.

So they all set out gaily to the Haunted Tower. You could hear their raucous voices echoing across the snow.

14. Night in the Haunted Tower

BEAVER HATEMAN and his companions could soon see, looming up in the distance, the enormous black bulk of the Haunted Tower.

But before they reached it they heard singing in the distance.

'That'll be the Respectable Horses,' said Hateman. 'They always go round on Christmas Eve.'

They soon came up with a group of three horses who were carol-singing outside the house of a man called Lilac Stamper.

He had a board fastened in front of his window on which were these words:

```
All singing prohibited.
Mr Stamper is writing a book.
```

```
He wishes for silence.
You sing at your own risk!
Stamper has publicly thrashed
three ballad singers, and has
caned four flute players.
He will do it again!
THIS MEANS YOU!
```

In spite of this menacing notice they kept on singing, and they were singing very badly.

These horses are called the Respectable Horses as they always look so neat and tidy, and they are great friends of Uncle's. They would have been to see him that night, but they were too busy singing in aid of a Home for Retired Horses. It's wonderful to see how smooth and black their coats are. Near the throat they have a patch of white almost like a clergyman's collar, and they always have well-brushed hooves.

They do not like Hateman, but they always treat him respectfully, and, strange to say, he never attacks them. In fact, he sometimes takes their part.

That evening, for instance, although longing for a fight, Hateman went up to them and said:

'If Stamper attacks you, I'll thrash him!'

The Respectable Horses nodded, but did not interrupt their singing, which was really painful. Horses cannot be said to have good voices, and theirs were particularly dull and heavy. Still, they managed a few good notes now and then.

Beaver Hateman waited.

By and by Stamper's window opened, and his thin white face appeared. He handed out two pound notes which the leader of the Respectable Horses put into a tin which was tied round his neck. Then he closed the window.

Beaver Hateman was mystified.

'Why didn't he attack you?' he said.

'Oh, Mr Hateman,' said the eldest of the horses, 'I'm afraid you didn't read the little footnote appended to Mr Stamper's notice. It's in very small type. Let me lend you this quizzing-glass.'

The eldest of the Respectable Horses carried an old-fashioned but powerful quizzing-glass suspended round his neck by a black ribbon.

Hateman took the glass.

'Where's the footnote?' he said.

The horse (whose name, by the way, was Mayhave Crunch) pointed to what looked like a greyish smudge on one corner of the notice. When Hateman looked at it through the quizzing-glass he found that it was in that very small type in which people sometimes print a whole page of writing in the space of a thumbnail. It read as follows:

```
Singers  are  however  allowed  to
perform on the following dates: Jan
1 to Dec 31 inclusive and on all
public holidays.
```

Hateman was indignant.

'The little skunk!' he said. 'He's tricking us!' He tried to get Stamper to come out, but Stamper smiled and stayed by his cosy little fire eating roasted chestnuts, and as his window had been well rubbed with Babble Trout Oil it could not be broken, and the Hateman gang had to leave him alone.

Beaver Hateman was just going away when Mayhave Crunch jingled a money-box under his nose.

Hateman felt in his pocket, and drew out a handful of bad money, brass sovereigns, lead half-crowns and very badly forged bank notes. At the bottom was a single good halfpenny, which he took out and gave to them.

They thanked him gravely, and passed on.

At last the Hateman gang arrived at the Haunted Tower.

As they opened the front door, a spectre leered at them, beckoned down a passage and then ran off. They went down the passage and arrived in a kind of hotel lounge. The walls were mildewed and hung with spiders' webs and the carpet was rat-eaten. There was a general air of decay and misery.

At a shabby reception desk stood a tall, cadaverous man.

He gave a loud shriek when he saw them, and pointed to two moth-eaten posters which hung side by side behind the desk.

One of them was headed:

BEFORE VISITING THE HAUNTED BEDROOMS

It showed a fat, prosperous-looking man walking along with a smile.

The other was headed:

AFTER VISITING THE BEDROOMS

It showed a lean miserable man with grey hair and his body bent almost double.

There was also a notice:

> When visiting leave your valuables with the clerk. He will endeavour to return the same, but does not promise to do so every time.

'Hand over the keys,' said Hateman.

'One key for the lot,' said the clerk in a false, rattling voice.

He seemed to be fumbling about with the key. At last he handed it to Hateman on a small tray. The moment Hateman got hold of it he dropped it. It was red-hot.

It's a good thing that Beaver Hateman's hands are covered with thick horny skin. He burnt the outside surface, but did not hurt himself at all. Hateman didn't waste much time with the miserable clerk. A bucket of coal happened to be standing near. He picked it up and emptied it over him.

They went on to find the rooms. Beaver Hateman fancied one that was labelled:

> HAUNTED ROOM NUMBER 52314567 A15/J.A.I.
> THE WHITE TERROR

Nailrod Hateman took

> NUMBER 52314568 A15/J.A.I.
> THE REMORSEFUL DUELLIST

Hitmouse said he would take

> NUMBER 52314569 A15/J.A.I.
> THE WAILING MURDERER AND CHAIN DRAGGER

Beaver and Nailrod went in, but Hitmouse, as you'll remember, is timid.

What he did was to wait till the others had gone in, and then lie down on the mat outside, where he thought he would be free from ghosts. He's never quite easy about ghosts, though they have all got used to them at Badfort, as Hootman every now and then has a ghostly friend over to see him.

But Hitmouse wanted to have the credit for being bold, and still to have a good night's rest. He wrapped himself up in the mat, and was just falling asleep when Beaver Hateman pushed open his door and came out to look for him.

'I say, Hitmouse,' he said, 'haven't you turned in yet? Well, you'd better come in here. The White Terror is an absolute wash-out, a very small ghost only about a foot high, and I'm not going to waste my time with it; I'm going into a room where there's something really terrific! Come on!'

Hitmouse didn't want to go, but Hateman took him by the collar and slung him in.

Once in the room, he could see nothing at first, and finding the bed comfortable he got into it, and was just falling asleep when he heard a low groan, and saw a very small ghost standing on a bedside table.

It stood there muttering:

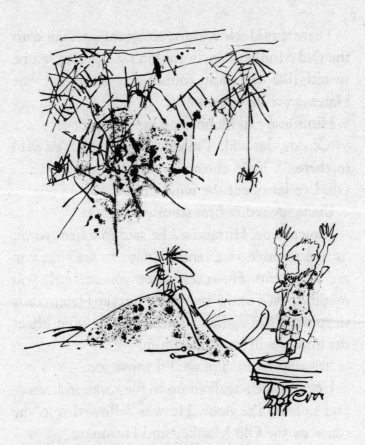

'I did it! I took the strawberry jam!'

It began to scream in a small voice.

Hitmouse tried to stick a skewer into it, but as it was made of something like thick fog, this was no good. All at once he felt terrified of the little figure, and darted out of bed into the passage.

What he saw reassured him.

There was Uncle coming along the passage with the Old Monkey. Uncle couldn't sleep, and felt he would like to walk round and see what the Hateman tribe were doing.

Hitmouse ran blubbering up to him.

'Oh, sir,' he said, 'I'm glad to see you. It's awful in there. A little ghost, a rotten little ghost! . . . Oh, I've fairly got the wind up!'

Uncle looked at him sternly.

'Cowardice, Hitmouse,' he said in a firm voice, 'is a detestable vice, and I grieve to see that you are its victim. However, since you are out, you might as well show us where Beaver Hateman is sleeping. I am rather anxious to see what effect the ghosts will have upon him.'

'It's two rooms up, sir. I'll show you.'

Uncle gravely walked up to the room indicated, and opened the door. He was followed into the room by the Old Monkey and Hitmouse.

He could not help smiling at the scene. The room was lit by a very small lamp in the shape of a skull. There was an enormous bed hung with black velvet curtains, and right in the middle of it snored Beaver Hateman. He was asleep, and his great boots, studded with iron nails, projected over the bottom rail.

Standing at the foot of the bed was a tall thin ghost, with a puzzled expression on his face. His hand held a sword, and every now and then he groaned, took the sword by the middle, and tried to stab himself.

Beaver Hateman snored on.

After a while another ghost appeared, dragging a chain with iron weights attached. The noise made by this spectre was terrific, but it had hardly any effect on Beaver Hateman. He stirred in his sleep for a moment, and then shouted:

'Easy with the kegs. Don't rumble them over the floor like that, or you'll start the staves!'

By this time several more ghosts had arrived, and the room began to get crowded. They took not the slightest notice of Uncle and the Old Monkey, but directed their attention to Hateman, who was now gurgling in his sleep and grinding his teeth a little.

By and by another ghost arrived, carrying with him a pan of blue fire, which made things in the room a little lighter. They hadn't noticed him before. He was trying to wash his hands, and moaning. Nobody, not even the other ghosts, took much notice of him, so he went farther into the corner as if disappointed, and began to wring his hands quietly.

However, the most terrifying spectre of the lot was now appearing. A door opened in the wall, and out stepped a fierce-looking phantom, with skulls and crossbones round its neck and carrying a great axe in its bony hand. With this ghost were a couple of others, carrying a block, then two more, conveying a prisoner.

They made the ghostly prisoner kneel down. He gave a cry for mercy, but down came the great axe, and his head rolled into a basket. Hateman partly woke up at this, gave a yawn that rattled the windows, then muttered, as he dropped off to sleep again:

'That looks like old Uncle going his round!'

He then began to snore louder than ever. He had rolled round till his head was over the edge of the bed, and with his great teeth showing he presented a somewhat fearful spectacle himself. The ghosts appeared to think so too, for they wavered and grew more and more insubstantial. At last one of them stepped forward and began to wail. His voice was piercing, and so strident that they all had to stop their ears. But it had little effect on Beaver Hateman. He is thoroughly used to screaming, for Hitmouse often sleeps in his room at Badfort, and, having a really bad conscience, regularly screams in his sleep.

So, when the spectre began to wail, Hateman took no notice at first. At last, when it yelled till the whole place shook, he stopped snoring for a moment, half lifted his head, and said in his sleep:

'Hitmouse, if you don't stop yelling, I'll . . .' Then his sleep became even more heavy, and his snoring settled down to a deep steady drone. His head, which was hanging out of bed, sank till it rested on a small stool at the bedside. This compressed his throat, and the noise he began to make then was simply unbearable.

The ghosts faded away till they were all gone.

Uncle and his companions stepped out of the room too. Uncle was secretly laughing.

They went down the corridor, and entered Nailrod Hateman's room. He wasn't asleep, but was watching an old ghost, who was trying vainly to pick up a phantom sovereign from a crack in the floor.

'That's your two hundred and seventeenth attempt, old lad!' Nailrod said cheerfully. 'And remember, when you've got it, it's no good. You can't spend it! Ha! Ha! Ha!'

The old ghost, however, took no notice of him, and began to grope again in the crack.

'Well, I must say, you're very persevering!' said Nailrod Hateman.

Just then he looked up and saw Uncle standing in the doorway.

'Hallo!' he said. 'Come and watch. It's a case of "If at first you don't succeed, try, try, try again!" It reminds me of those yarns you used to tell us about how you succeeded in business.'

Uncle was in no mood for controversy, or even reproof. He simply gave Nailrod Hateman a searching, severe glance and moved on.

They found Hootman in the passage in a very bad temper. He had gone to a room farther down with the title:

BATTLE OF ALL THE SPECTRES

AND

THE STRANGLING WIZARD

He had been most disappointed, for no ghost had appeared at all. The fact is, ghosts look on Hootman as partly one of themselves and they detest him so much that not one of them will go near him, except the one or two who visit him at

Badfort, and these are ghosts who have been driven out of the tower.

The consequence was that he had been awake for the best part of the night in a damp room with nobody to talk to.

By now, it was time for Uncle to go home, so they set out. They arrived safely, and had a late sleep on Christmas morning. So did the Badfort crowd. It was nearly twelve o'clock when they turned up for lunch.

'How did you sleep?' said Uncle to Beaver Hateman.

'Oh, very well indeed, undisturbed by ghosts or anything else!'

The Hateman tribe always go away soon after dinner, because their comparatively good manners are by that time getting near breaking-point.

So when Beaver Hateman said he must be off, Uncle did not try to delay him.

'Well, goodbye, Uncle. Are the sledges of provisions ready?'

The sledges were ready, but Uncle did not like the tone of this remark. It took his valuable presents too much for granted, so he said gravely:

'The sledges *are* ready, but I wish you would have the common civility to say "Thank you"!'

'Oh, stow it, Uncle. You owe us something. You know jolly well that you'd be bored stiff if we didn't have a dust-up occasionally! Well, goodbye, and remember this: that the next time we meet you'll get something to make you look less pleased with yourself!'

15. The Sweet Tower

CHRISTMAS had not been over very long before much hammering and knocking was heard to come from Badfort. In spite of this Uncle decided to take a little time off to go exploring.

'I'm running short of sweets,' he said, 'and I'd like to know what is in that big green tower at the back. I've looked at my plan, and it said: "Tower Number 279A; Sweet Store and Chocolate Warehouse. Servitor in charge: Samuel Hardbake." I've never seen Hardbake yet, and I thought we might have a good look round and bring back a supply of eatables.'

They all approved of this and Uncle said they needn't carry much stuff, only a few baskets. They had very hard work to get the One-Armed

Badger to travel light, but they got off at last, Uncle, the Old Monkey, Gubbins, the One-Armed Badger and Whitebeard. They didn't want to take Whitebeard much, but he begged hard to come, so at last they let him.

So far as they could make out from the plan, the way to get to Sweet Tower was to take the circular railway to Lion Tower, then change on to a sliding chute to Swan Tower, walk across the top, where there's a spring machine that shoots you up to a little brown tower only thirty storeys high, then from the top of that tower there's an escalator to Merry-Go-Round Flat, a place where there's a free fun fair always going. Then you get to the Black Stag tunnel and ride on trolleys for about a mile, go up the elevator, turn to the right, then on to the big swing boats which swing you on to Buzzard Tower. After that it's easy.

In one corner of Buzzard Tower there was a little rusty switchback railway labelled 'To Sweet Tower'. It hardly looked as though it would work at all, but it started right off with a scream, tearing down culverts and jumping great chasms at such a speed that you could hardly see anything. The journey only lasted about half a minute. Then it ran suddenly into a wall of what looked like soap, and stopped. When they looked back, and saw right in the distance the dim outline of Buzzard Tower, they began to realize how far they had come.

It was Sweet Tower all right.

There in his office at the entrance was Samuel Hardbake, busily entering up some items in his ledger.

He looked up as they came.

'What's this!' he said. 'Visitors ain't allowed except on the third Friday of every second month. That's today, and the boys from Dr Lyre's school are here already. My hands will be full up with them, so you can take yourselves off.'

'Wait a bit,' said Uncle. 'I am Uncle, the owner of this place.'

'Oh, are you? I have my doubts. Let's have a look at you.'

He put on another pair of spectacles and looked at Uncle for a long time, comparing his figure with a framed portrait that was hanging in the office.

'Well, you look a bit like him,' he said reluctantly; 'but what about these fellows?' He glanced at Whitebeard. 'I don't like the look of your companions. Mind, if you take any sweets away you must sign for them, whoever you are.'

'By the way,' said Uncle, 'you referred just now to a visit from Dr Lyre's boys. I never gave them permission to come.'

'Oh, didn't you? Then what's the meaning of this?'

He reached from his desk a paper with Uncle's crest on the top. It stated that Dr Lyre's boys were to be allowed to view the Sweet Tower and that each boy was to be permitted to take away as many sweets as he could carry. It was signed in Uncle's flourishing hand.

'This is a forgery,' said Uncle sternly. 'Well, I think we'd better go into the tower, and when the Doctor comes I'll have a word with him.'

The tower was a wonderful place, with hundreds of rooms all filled with coconut ice, toffee, mint rock and every kind of chocolate.

They paused in a great hall which was walled with toffee and floored with slab chocolate. While they were looking round they heard a sound of cheering, and Dr Lyre appeared at the head of his boys.

Uncle asked him the meaning of the permit.

'Why, it was this way,' said the Doctor; 'an inspector called in at the school the other day and said that he had been sent by you to inspect the boys. He heard the top form read, and then he took the chalk and wrote a sentence on the blackboard for them to read. A strange sentence it seemed to me. It was this:

UNCLE IS A BOASTER!

'I expostulated of course, but –'

'Stop!' shouted Uncle. 'The abominable sentence you have quoted gives me the key to the identity of this so-called inspector. What did he look like?'

'Oh, he was rather roughly dressed. He wore a sack suit, I think. All the same, I rather liked him: I'm just a shade deaf, but I think he said his name was Hateman. I know he told me you had appointed him to be an inspector.'

'All right!' said Uncle, with a hissing intake of breath. 'I begin to see how things stand, but go on, I might as well hear the whole disgraceful story. What did he do then?'

'I asked him to lunch, and for an inspector he had an abnormally large appetite, but he liked my book about Lion Tower, and took a couple of copies.'

'Did he pay you for them?'

'Why no, not at the time. He said he would send me a cheque for five pounds the next day, but it hasn't come yet. I expect he's a bit absent-minded like myself.'

Uncle smiled bitterly.

'Then,' continued the Doctor, 'he was so pleased with the boys' reading that he gave the school a month's holiday there and then. He also said that he would get you to send a letter giving the boys permission to visit the Sweet Tower, and take away a sackful each. The letter arrived next day. It was brought by a curious little chap about the size of Noddy Ninety. His name, he said, was Mr Isidore Hitmouse.'

'Very good,' said Uncle sternly. 'Call the boys together; I will have a word with the whole school before they inspect the tower.'

They were soon drawn up, and awaited Uncle's speech with eager faces.

Uncle was very grave. For some time he looked over the ranks of boys with a far-away but sombre expression. At last he spoke.

'Boys,' he said, 'I am sorry to inform you that you are here today under a forged permit, a permit deliberately made out by a man so grey in sin, that it seems barely possible that such a person

should exist at all. He has now added forgery to his other misdeeds, and above all he is trying to be generous at another person's expense. However, I will settle with him later, and now, so that you may see that my liberality exceeds even that of a forger, who does not own what he gives away, I will arrange for you to receive not one but two sacks of sweets today, and I will also write out a permit whereby the whole school shall visit Merry-Go-Round Flats free of charge.'

There was terrific cheering as Uncle announced this, and afterwards they all went right through the Sweet Tower. It's full of surprises.

'Not a bad place,' said Uncle, as he sat down for a moment on a divan made of mint rock, and looked through a barley-sugar window into an interior courtyard paved with glacier mints.

'I think it's lovely,' said the Old Monkey in a rapturous voice. 'Oh, look at that man. He's bringing chocolates in a wheelbarrow to mend that hole in the pavement!'

They were rather amused, when they arrived at a big hall at the very top, to find Noddy Ninety was playing cricket. He had brought his bat and set up three big sticks of mint rock as wickets. Some of the boys were bowling at him with aniseed drops the size of cricket balls. He hit them every time into the same place, a huge sack which hung from the hand of a chocolate man. When the sack was full, the man, who was on a pedestal, overbalanced and fell with a resounding smash.

Old Whitebeard had been quietly eyeing a presentation box of chocolates with the intention of sticking it away under his beard, but, just as he was lifting his arm, Noddy Ninety sent down a very fast aniseed ball, and caught him on the elbow. It jarred his funnybone, and he thought it best to retire quietly to the background.

After that they went up to the boiled-sweet room. This is a perfectly enormous place right at the top of the tower. A cascade of hard sweets of all colours, red, green and blue, came pouring out of a spout, and made a beautiful rainbow-coloured pool on the floor. They all gathered sackfuls from time to time.

After that they went to the Fun Fair, and then returned home, everybody in a very satisfied state of mind, especially Doctor Lyre, for Uncle ordered five copies of his book about Lion Tower, and paid for them on the spot.

But their satisfaction was short-lived.

As they neared Homeward they heard a low clanking hum, and an aeroplane appeared from behind Badfort and flew towards them. Rudolph, who was out near the moat, was already running for his crossbow.

It was a miserable and rusty plane, and seemed to cough and hesitate in the air. A number of tins of petrol were loosely tied on with rope. Beaver Hateman seemed to be flying it. Rudolph tried to shoot it down, but though he peppered the figure in the front seat with many bolts from his crossbow, the plane still came on, dripping oil and making a creaking noise.

They found out afterwards that the figure of Beaver Hateman was a dummy, and that Hitmouse was really flying it, crouched in the rear seat and using a dual control.

The dummy fell out just as the plane was flying off, and they found that it had been hit in nineteen places. Not one of Rudolph's shots had missed. When the plane arrived overhead, a shower of leaflets fell out, also a large bomb, filled with glue, ink, and tin-tacks, but luckily it fell in the moat.

They picked up one of the leaflets which read as follows:

TO ALL FREE CITIZENS:

This is to announce that we have at last completed our plans against Uncle, the arch-bully, tyrant and boaster. WATCH HIM! His grandeur will fade.

WATCH HIM!

Uncle made the Old Monkey gather up all these pamphlets and burn them.

He was uneasy, however, and after a time he said:

'Cowgill tells me the helicopter he's been working on is so improved that he can take me up

now. Some of us will go over to Badfort, hover a little and see what they're up to.'

In fact only one person could go with Uncle, for he is rather heavy, and Cowgill, who had made the helicopter and understood it, was the best one to go.

They took off from the top of the tower in which Uncle lives, and soon they were almost stationary, and, thanks to Cowgill's ENGINE NOISE MODIFIER, almost silent in the air above Badfort.

Uncle forgot the danger of an occasional arrow and took no notice of the one or two duck bombs which were catapulted up at them from a wooden erection which looked like a see-saw. This was a unique experience, this view of the enemy fortress from the air.

'Badfort is hollow!' he said in surprise to Cowgill. 'Those towers in front are entirely deceptive. Why, what an untidy-looking place it is with that shabby field in the middle and the rickety galleries running all the way round. Can you go a little lower, Cowgill, I want to see what those offices are at the side.'

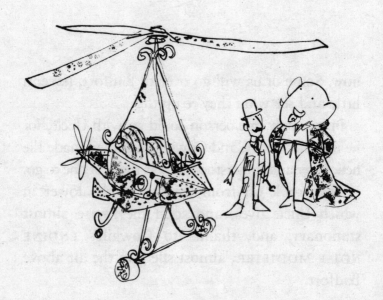

'It's not safe to lose much more height, sir,' said Cowgill.

'Oh, rubbish!' said Uncle, who was too interested to feel danger. 'Why, I do believe they are moneylenders' offices! So that is where they get their cash!'

'There's Flabskin coming out with a bag of money!' said Cowgill.

'You're right! And as for pawnshops, Cowgill, there must be at least a hundred of them. Look at the degraded wretches streaming in with sack suits and hating-books!'

'And there's a place where you can pawn yourself, sir,' said Cowgill.

'What do you mean, pawn yourself, Cowgill?'

'Oh, I've heard a lot about that,' said Cowgill. 'It's an old Badfort custom. A man can go in and get ten shillings on himself, and then go and sit on a shelf as a pledge.'

'But what does he do with the money?'

'The usual thing, I believe, is to send out for a keg of Black Tom, sir, and sit on the shelf drinking it.'

'Disgraceful,' said Uncle, adding hastily, 'but what then?'

'I believe he throws the keg at the proprietor, and escapes!'

'Atrocious behaviour,' said Uncle. 'Pass me the glass, Cowgill, and go a little lower if possible; I want to read the menu outside that café.'

'No lower, sir, I dare not risk it!' said Cowgill.

'I can just read it!' cried Uncle, leaning perilously out in his excitement: 'Gossip Muffin, ½d., Envy Jelly, 1d., Cruelty Sausage, ½d., and Muddle Jelly, ½d.! What an atrocious list of comestibles!'

'Shall I gain height now, sir?' said Cowgill, looking anxious.

'One moment!' said Uncle, sharply. 'What is that long wooden building on wheels behind Badfort? It looks like a Noah's Ark! That's what they've been hammering at.'

'Look out, sir,' shouted Cowgill.

A yell of derision came up from one of the dusty galleries below and a dart whistled close past Uncle's trunk. The shock made Uncle tip perilously forward. For one frightful second it looked as if nothing could save him from pitching right into the crowd which had collected below. The lurching of the helicopter was sickening, but Cowgill was able to control the machine with an effort and Uncle righted himself, breathing heavily. He and Cowgill looked at each other, acknowledging the full horror of what they had just escaped.

'Let us return to Homeward,' said Uncle with as much dignity as he could command; 'I have seen enough. Those are the people who wish to depose me! I need say no more!'

16. The Danger

'WELL,' said 'Uncle the next day, yawning, 'no hammering from Badfort today! It's pleasant to be quiet for a bit, but I almost miss the miserable oafs. If some of them would turn up I'd be able to sift this matter of the school inspector and the Sweet Tower.'

He picked up a duck bomb, which somebody had left behind on Christmas Eve, and skimmed it over to Badfort. There was no reply. Nobody seemed to be there.

'Where are they?' he said pettishly to the Old Monkey.

It was a dull morning. Not a single letter came and there were no callers except a thin man who was trying to sell a skeleton key guaranteed to open any door in Homeward. Uncle sent him off with a big bag of bananas. Rudolph was wolf-hunting at the back of Homeward; it's very nice out there, and has never been really explored. There are some mysterious green lights at night that have often puzzled Uncle, but he is still too busy trying to get the hang of his own house to spend time on them.

Cloutman was writing an interminable letter, holding the pen in his great fist as if it were a pistol. Alonzo S. Whitebeard was dozing on the sofa, secretly counting over the coins in his pocket.

Everything felt flat.

'What are those rascals doing?' asked Uncle again. 'That big portable building intrigues me, I must say.'

Just then Captain Walrus came in.

'Good morning, sir,' he said. 'I want to tell you that our neighbours are up to no good. I passed Joe's on the way to Cheapman's this morning, and they were all laughing about something. He's got some new stuff called 'Scream Fizz', which is very popular. But they can't even sit down and drink their vile brew decently. They all stand round and scream in chorus:

'He stole my glass of scream fizz
Once but never again.
He came with laughter on his lips
And went away with pain.'

'Oh, they're a set of scoundrels! But some of them can sing properly if they want to. They've got a chap there called Sigismund Hateman, who is a really splendid singer. He's going to sing this afternoon in the field in front of Badfort, and they tell me that people are coming from all parts to hear him.'

Uncle was deeply interested in this account. He also felt very much puzzled. What could they be up to? Instead of attacking Homeward they were singing. It seemed very strange. Uncle scratched his head as he tried to understand it.

At last he spoke to Captain Walrus.

'Where did you say this singer was going to perform?'

'In the big field over there, and he's going to start just after lunch. You can see the people rolling up already.'

It was true. Thousands of badgers were streaming over the plain, and a great company of idlers from Wolftown were already there.

Uncle ordered dinner, and afterwards said:

'Well, you can all go and hear the star Sigismund if you like. I'll stay here.'

The Old Monkey's eyes shone. He loves singing, and he loves being in a tightly packed crowd, because he runs over the heads of the people to the front row. They try to catch him, but are all too tightly wedged, and he enjoys the sensation.

'It's very good of you to let us go, sir,' he said gratefully.

'No, it isn't,' replied Uncle. 'I don't want you here while you are longing to go and hear that traitor sing, and I don't want to hear his wretched singing myself. You can all clear out.'

There's a kind of mud pond at the edge of the moat and when there's nobody about Uncle loves to wallow in it. He doesn't do it when anyone is there, because he thinks he would be made fun of.

They all set off and left him, and as soon as they were well over the drawbridge Uncle took off his purple dressing-gown, and walked down to the mud pond. Nobody was about, so he plunged in, and wallowed blissfully in the warm mud. He spent about an hour in this way, and was just having a pleasant doze on the bank, when he heard tremendous cheering in the distance.

In spite of himself, he got up and climbed to the moat bank. Right in front of him was a meadow shaded by trees. In it were gathered an enormous crowd of people. Standing in the midst of them, on a large barrel, was Sigismund Hateman.

Sigismund began to sing. From where he was standing, Uncle found to his annoyance that he could not hear a word, only just the faintest whisper of a tune.

The song ended. Then came the mightiest outburst of cheering that Uncle had heard for a long time. Everybody listened eagerly and all appeared to have forgotten their quarrel. Then there was a dead silence, and Uncle could see the Old Monkey running to and fro over the people's heads.

The next song was a quiet one. Uncle could hardly hear it at all. He began to feel much annoyed. He looked round. There was still nobody about, so he felt he could safely leave the castle. He strolled quietly over the drawbridge, and began to walk towards the crowd, keeping in the shadow of the bushes and trees. At last he came near enough to hear.

Sigismund Hateman was just finishing a Spanish song about a sick goat tormented by wasps. He sang it very sadly. His subject was not promising, yet Uncle found himself sniffing, and two large tears fell down on each side of his trunk. Everyone seemed to be touched; even Beaver Hateman pulled out an old dishcloth which served him as a handkerchief, and gave a loud sneeze.

There seemed to be no end to Sigismund's repertoire of songs; he sang tragic, narrative and

comic songs, one after the other; and it was a
tribute to him that so mixed a crowd kept dead
still in order to hear him.

He announced his subjects before he sang them.
All at once, he gave out in his high speaking voice:
'My next song is a comic parody of "The Village
Blacksmith".' Then he began to sing:

> 'Under a spreading chestnut tree,
> The village tyrant stands;
> Uncle, a mighty man is he,
> With large and sinewy hands,
> And the muscles of his waving trunk,
> Are strong as iron bands.

'*Week in, week out, from morn till night,*
You can hear his boastings blow,
You can see him swing his loaded trunk
With measured beat and slow,
And he often kicks his neighbours up
When the evening sun is low.

'*Lying, swindling and boasting,*
Onward through life he goes;
Each morning sees some crime begun,
Each evening sees its close;
Somebody bullied, somebody done,
Has earned a night's repose.'

When Uncle heard this song he was full of indignation, but he thought it best to go away quietly, so he stole back to the house. About ten minutes later, the concert broke up, and his followers hurried away, and managed to get back before they were attacked. The moment they arrived, Uncle asked:

'How did you enjoy the concert?'

'Oh, it was grand,' they all said.

'I happened to be walking near, during the last item,' said Uncle gravely, 'and I want to say this once and for all, I'm profoundly disappointed in the lot of you. You listened to that abominable song and liked it! Now it's no use your saying you didn't, and it's most disloyal of you! Whitebeard, I was going to give you threepence this afternoon, but you can go without it! As for you, sir –' he turned to the Old Monkey – 'you actually ran over people's heads to hear an insulting song about your master!'

'I didn't know it was about you, sir. He announced it as "The Village Tyrant".'

'Then you ought to have come right away, the moment you heard the first lines, but there, I've given up all hope of finding decency or loyalty anywhere!'

Just then the Young Monkey came up, stuttering. He pointed to the window.

They looked out and Uncle saw the large portable building which had reminded him of a Noah's Ark being brought out from behind Badfort. It was about a hundred feet long, and fifty broad, and was being pulled along by as motley a crew as ever tugged a weight. More than a hundred persons were drawing on the ropes. Beaver Hateman, mounted on the Wooden-Legged Donkey, was the leader, and behind him were all the principal inhabitants of Badfort, assisted by a mixed crowd of captive badgers and others.

When they had dragged the building out into the meadow where Sigismund had been singing, they nailed to the front of it a huge sign:

PLEASURELAND CINEMA
Continuous Performance. Come in thousands!

The booking office was opened, and at once a crowd of badgers filled the place. From Homeward they could hear shrieks and squeaks of mirth from the building. At the end of every half-hour small doors were opened at the side of the building, and the spectators were driven out, for they were reluctant to leave so soon.

Most of them paid another halfpenny to see the next part of the film. It was only a halfpenny to go in, but it really cost much more, for everyone was driven out every half-hour. The film was called *The Unicorn's Dream* and it must have been really splendid. People who had been driven out could be seen borrowing money or even selling themselves into slavery to see another instalment; for you really paid quite a lot to see the whole thing.

The Old Monkey and the others were dying to go, but they dared not ask permission, so they spent the evening quietly in the large dining-room.

Uncle amused himself by showing one or two of his treasures to Alonzo S. Whitebeard, who loves to see things that are costly.

He opened a silver cupboard to show him a strange device. There was a golden spout, and from it there continually dropped shillings. They fell with a jingling sound into a little wooden keg mounted on rails. When the keg was full, automatic machinery took it away, and another one came up in its place, while the old one moved away to the treasury. These shillings represented the annual rents continually coming in from a gigantic tower away at the far end of Uncle's castle. They were collected by a trusty agent called Oliver Hoot, and just to show you how vast are Uncle's holdings I may mention that he has never yet seen Hoot, nor inspected the tower, which is called Goldfish Lodge. He means to go some day soon, but the way there is hard and puzzling, so he's waiting till Oliver Hoot comes to show him over.

Meanwhile the rents keep coming in through a tube. He actually gave Whitebeard a peep at his treasury through a twelve-inch-thick glass window protected by a flame thrower. They looked into an enormous room built of solid steel six feet thick. He only gave him one peep, but Whitebeard saw the flash and dazzle of diamonds, and the milky radiance of pearls set off by the red fire of rubies. He felt a bit dazzled, and couldn't see clearly.

Uncle, growing tired, said:

'I think I'll go out for a short walk. You can all amuse yourselves round the fire. I don't want anyone to come with me, not even the Old Monkey.'

Before he left, he gave the Old Monkey a two-shilling piece, for he seemed surprised at Uncle going out without him, and was downhearted.

Uncle set out. It was getting late, and all the people had gone. It seemed a very good time to have a look at the Pleasureland Cinema.

17. The Disaster

WHEN Uncle came to the door of the cinema, everything was perfectly quiet. He waited a bit, but there seemed to be nobody about, so he decided to go in. There were some little windows high up which gave a dim light, but he drew out an electric torch from his pocket and snapped it on.

It looked very much like any other cinema, only smaller. There were some rather expensive seats labelled twopence and right in the middle of them there was a monster armchair marked threepence. Uncle went and sat down in it, and looked at the screen. It had a curtain over it, on which were some strange pictures, but he couldn't make out what they were in that dim light. One seemed to be of a wharf with boats. As he leaned forward for a closer look, he heard a sudden snap behind him, and a harsh voice shouted:

'Got him at last!'

Uncle jumped up, and rushed to the door of the cinema. It was closed and locked, but he thought little of that. He knew well that with his trunk and tusks he could soon demolish a flimsy door like this one. He threw his weight on the door, and it began to give. Another good push, and it yielded altogether.

Then came the sinister surprise.

Outside the door there was a great network of solid steel bars, and beyond these he saw the leering, hideous face of Beaver Hateman.

'Ha! Ha! Uncle,' said the latter. 'We've got you at last. You can try as hard as you like, but you won't get out of this!'

Uncle snorted with fury, and made a mad-bull rush at the flimsy side of the cinema. To his surprise, the wooden walls were backed by solid steel.

Again and again he rushed, but in vain. Then he rushed at the screen. To his surprise and horror, this covered a solid iron wall.

At last, with jarred tusks and bruised limbs, he came furiously back, and sat down in the threepenny armchair.

Meanwhile, Beaver Hateman was busy taking down the wooden doors, and opening others at the sides. Then he gave a bubbling howl, which was his rallying cry, and all at once his followers appeared.

Nailrod and his father, Hitmouse, Mud-Dog, Mallet Crackbone, Sigismund Hateman, Flabskin and all the others were there. Hootman hovered at one of the side doors.

They carried with them crossbows, duck bombs, skewers and bladders of vinegar.

When they saw Uncle, they all began to howl and shout with delight.

Uncle was reassured, for he knew that the noise would soon bring his own followers up, and in this he was right. There was a loud whistle from Homeward, and Rudolph, the Old Monkey, Cloutman, Gubbins, and the rest poured over the drawbridge. They left Cowgill and the Old Monkey's father, however, to defend the house. Captain Walrus also came, trailing behind, laden almost to the ground with marlinspikes and belaying-pins.

'Let's knock the swine out,' shouted Cloutman
as he ran.

'Ay, that we will!' replied the Captain. 'I shan't
be happy till I use every one of these belaying-pins
on those pirates!'

'Let me get hold of Beaver Hateman,' said Gubbins, extending his mighty arms, 'and I'll hug him till he squeaks for mercy!'

They were quite near the cinema, when Beaver Hateman shouted out to them:

'We've got old Uncle, and there is a stone weighing ten tons over his head. If one of you throws a spike or a belaying-pin, down comes that stone and Uncle is flattened!'

'Is that true, sir?' shouted Gubbins, who was the nearest to the cinema.

Uncle looked up.

To his horror he saw that the whole roof of the cinema was composed of a great stone suspended by a single chain, and this chain, in turn, was fastened to an immensely strong rope. By the side of the rope, with a sharp sword in his flabby paw, stood Jellytussle.

It's seldom that Jellytussle speaks, but just then he looked down and said in an oily but cruel voice:

'It's true, Uncle! One slash and you're flattened out!'

Uncle is cool in emergencies, though inclined to be irritable over ordinary annoyances. He called out to his followers:

'Do nothing for the present! I fear these miscreants are speaking the truth for once.'

'That's a nasty remark!' said Beaver Hateman savagely. 'But wait a bit, and you'll know what revenge means. However, I'm going to keep cool too for the present. No, friends, don't throw your duck bombs yet! Now, it's no good getting excited, Uncle. These are my terms.

'A MILLION POUNDS! No less. I've gone into debt over this binge. I've raised all the money I could to buy this cage and the biggest dump of Black Tom and food ever known to celebrate. I've sold myself as a slave to nine different people to raise the cash. If Uncle produces a million pounds, and also signs a statement to the effect that he stole a bicycle as the start of his fortunes, I'm inclined to say, "Treat him a bit rough and then let him go!" But, mind you, it must be a million pounds.'

He turned to his henchmen, who were gibbering with excitement. 'In the meantime, you can all have one shot each as a treat, just to show him what we're made of. Now all together!'

There was a hiss, and dozens of darts buried themselves in Uncle's hide, and at the same time he was deluged in poisoned vinegar. Meanwhile a deafening shriek arose from his tormentors.

'I can't stand this!' cried Cloutman. 'We must attack!'

'If you do,' said Beaver Hateman, 'down comes the stone!'

It was no good, they had to wait.

Meanwhile, Uncle drew out as many of the darts as he could. Pierced, insulted and streaming with vinegar, he was yet an imposing sight.

At last he stood up and waved his hand for silence. As he stared haughtily round the circle of bandits, they all felt small for the moment.

Then he spoke.

'I must say,' he said, 'I thought you had reached the bottom of human iniquity. Now I see that I am mistaken. It is like looking into a loathsome tank. You see one form of horror and think, "That's the worst!" and then there's a slight stirring of the turbid fluid, and another form, more monstrous, more –'

'Shut up!' shouted Beaver Hateman. 'We don't want a speech! Will you pay the million pounds or not? Now, out with it, or down comes the stone!'

Uncle paused. He was in a difficult predicament. The question was, would they liberate him if they got the money? He waited gloomily, lashing himself with his trunk in painful thought.

Just then there came a loud report, and a crimson flare lit up the sky behind them. There was a dismal screaming, and Flabskin rushed up shouting:

'The Black Tom dump's afire. Someone must have lit it!'

Meanwhile, huge flames were rising into the sky. It was true. The vast pile of kegs and baskets had been fired by someone, and now the whole place was radiant with the red glare. Beaver Hateman wavered. His desire to save the dump was so great that he was almost prepared to leave the cinema.

At last he shouted:

'Down with the stone, Jellytussle! Let's try to save the dump.'

But just as Jellytussle raised his sword to cut the rope, there was a twanging sound, and a well-aimed crossbow bolt knocked the weapon out of his hand. Rudolph had crept round to the back, and had been waiting for his opportunity.

Meanwhile the Old Monkey and Mig had managed to get an oxygen blowpipe at work on the bars behind the screen.

The tide had turned!

'Make a rush, sir!' shouted the Old Monkey. 'Just near the screen.'

Uncle did so, and in a moment found himself in the cool night air, free, and ready to deal out a terrible punishment. Trumpeting with fury, he turned on his tormentors.

They had all run away to the dump and were watching the burning kegs with cries of lamentation on their lips. It was impossible for them to get very near the dump because of the heat, and everything was as bright as day in the terrific glare.

Then, like a mighty avalanche, Uncle was upon them, and he was followed by Cloutman, Gubbins, Captain Walrus, Rudolph and the rest, while Alonzo S. Whitebeard followed close behind.

The Badfort crowd put up a most determined resistance, but nobody could stand before Uncle that night. Trampling with his feet, piercing with his tusks, lassoing with his trunk, he was a veritable tornado. Meanwhile Cloutman was singling out individuals and stunning them with one blow of his fist, while Old Walrus laid about him with belaying-pins and marlinspikes in true sea-dog fashion. The twang of Rudolph's crossbow seemed to be everywhere at once.

They got some very hard knocks themselves. Old Nailrod Hateman threw a keg of blazing Black Tom right over Gubbins and he had to rush into the water of the marsh to put the fire out. Uncle himself was half-blinded with vinegar and pierced with dozens of darts, but he seemed hardly to feel them.

At last he came face to face with Beaver Hateman. Uncle tried to kick him up, but his kick came at the wrong angle.

It merely sent him along the ground. He turned nineteen somersaults before he found his feet. He looked like a human wheel spinning along the ground. Just as he at last ceased his whirling, and stood for a moment to take a breath, Uncle saw his opportunity. There was a quick rush, and a sharp thud, a loud cry, and then the body of Beaver Hateman soared majestically into the crimson sky over the burning dump.

That was the end of the resistance. All the Badfort people faded away, and Uncle and his followers were left on the field triumphant.

They marched home, merely pausing to set the cinema on fire, and they soon crossed the drawbridge.

As they entered, Cowgill, who is a good trumpeter, blew a joyous blast.

They hurried into the hall. Hot baths were prepared, Magic Ointment was provided, medicine and bandages were made ready, and, only an hour after the great fight, Uncle was well-nigh himself again.

As he sat down, he said:

'Well, I think that's the best night's work I've ever done! Tomorrow shall be a day of public rejoicing!'

18. The Day of Public Rejoicing

THE next day dawned cloudless. It seemed as if all nature were prepared to revel with Uncle. The air was like crystal, except that in front of Badfort the dump was still burning and throwing up a great column of black smoke, which fortunately blew away from Uncle's and right over the top of the house of Hateman.

Uncle got up in high spirits. His wounds were nearly healed, and he spent the morning in receiving deputations, and also congratulatory telegrams from all parts of the country.

Many presents also arrived. The Marquis of Wolftown outdid himself, sending no less than a hundred trains filled with hams, lard, dried goats' flesh, etc. Cheapman sent an army of a thousand badgers, who marched in single file, each carrying on his head a box of provisions.

The King of the Badgers, poor as he was, had still managed to send six stalwart policemen carrying boxes of choice dates and fruits, as well as a little case containing some of his family jewellery. I may say that Uncle returned this, and with it such a handsome gift in cash that the King was quite well off for about a year after.

An unknown magnate called Rosco, who lives beyond the green lights in the marshes, sent a hundred wagon-loads of butter, and twenty kegs of first-grade water-melon pickle.

There was also an illuminated address, hastily prepared by the badgers, with a photo of Uncle, and three hundred and fourteen lines of praise.

They were going to finish up that night with a great festival banquet and a display of fireworks, but, in the meantime, Cowgill, that most ingenious man, had managed to make a vast supply of daylight fireworks. I don't know whether you have seen these, but they go up like rockets, then explode, making many very curious shapes in the sky.

Some of them made clouds like lions, some like unicorns, but the best of all were some huge

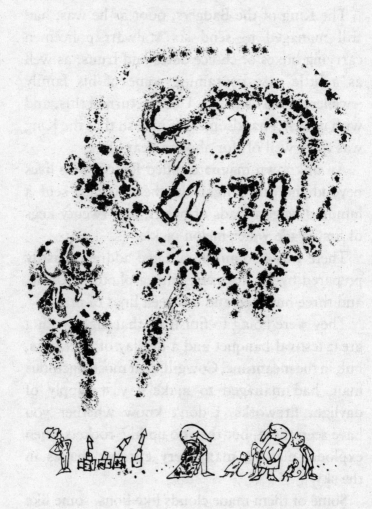

rockets, which when they exploded made a great pink cloud in the sky on which was the gigantic figure of an elephant, with uplifted trunk. These were loudly cheered.

During the day Uncle made preparations for a feast on the green in front of Homeward.

Decorations began to appear. The most remote towers were hung with silk curtains and flags.

Cowgill was in his element, for his staff of engineers were preparing an elaborate scheme of flood-lighting and illuminations. Right above Homeward, they were rushing up a monster sign: 'Uncle the Victor'. Bells rang, songs were shouted. The Old Monkey was particularly happy, because Uncle had told him that he never intended to go exploring without him again.

Butterskin Mute arrived about noon, driving a wagon loaded with ferns and beautiful flowers, and he was followed by about twenty farm carts loaded with his finest vegetables.

It took them nearly all day to make the preparations. Invitations were out early, and the railways and elevators were black with passengers coming to the feast.

Uncle had arranged for many jugglers and singers to be at hand to entertain the waiting crowds. Meanwhile the banqueting tables were being set out, and a huge festival chair of solid gold studded with turquoises had arrived from Cowgill's works.

They had very little to eat during the day: there was not much time. As soon as one deputation had gone, another appeared on the drawbridge. All the presents were piled up in one place. There was no attempt at order, they came so fast. You saw casks of lard, hams, Turkish delight, chests of tea, side by side with ornamental chairs, cups and goblets.

At last all was ready. Dr Lyre and his boys had come, and also Auntie and Miss Wace, the Maestro and the Little Lion. So had Don Guzman and the two leopards, the Respectable Horses, and the Old Man and Eva. Everybody was there.

At six o'clock in the evening the banquet began, and it continued till nine, when, at a signal from Uncle, the whole castle was illuminated by millions of electric lights while the great sign flashed above their heads in red, purple and yellow.

'This does me good,' said Uncle to the Old Monkey as he leaned back in his chair. He was wearing his diamond trunk-tips, and gold-studded boots, and a special purple dressing-gown embroidered with gold and rubies.

'I was never so happy in my life, sir,' said the Old Monkey, with glistening eyes. 'The main thing is that you're safe and sound!'

Uncle made no reply, but put his hand into his pocket and pressed a five-pound note into the Old Monkey's paw.

Then the fireworks began, and continued for more than an hour. They were stupendous. Some rockets were so huge that they seemed like barrels on the end of scaffolding poles. Then they burst in the air, turning the sky into a lake of dazzling light.

At last the fireworks were over, and Uncle began to distribute his gifts. He had decided that the whole pile should be given to the assembled multitudes, and, besides that, he had added a pound note for everyone, and an enormous sack of mixed foods and goods. So big were these sacks, that the dwarfs in particular found it impossible to move them, and had to hire transport.

At last the multitudes began to fade away, but before they went Uncle made a speech:

'Friends and followers,' he said, 'we are all assembled today to rejoice over the defeat of a set of human skunks. (*Loud cheers!*) I am very proud today, and yet, I am in a somewhat humble mood – so much happiness makes me feel almost solemn. I wish to say this, that I have today sent a cheque for £2,000 to the owner of the bicycle, which I once, in my callow youth, er – appropriated for my own temporary use. I have also sent him six hundred casks of herrings (*cheers*), a thousand kegs of Turkish delight (*loud cheers*), and fifty thousand first-grade cheeses! (*Terrific cheers!*) I think, after this,' said Uncle, mildly but firmly, 'that I shall hear no more of a certain song. Now disperse, and I hope to meet you all again on many occasions. Be upright, pay your rent, avoid brawling and disorder, and you will find Uncle a friend and protector at all times.'

As he ended, the cheering was deafening, but at last they began to go away, and Uncle sat down for a quiet chat with the Old Monkey.

Meanwhile at Badfort also a celebration was going on. Beaver Hateman had persuaded his followers that, in spite of being kicked up, he had scored a great victory over Uncle. Their stocks were low, but a Syrian, called Abdullah the Clothes-Peg Merchant, who lived in the marsh, had sent them presents. He sent them seven wagons loaded with dates and dried goats' flesh of an inferior quality and also he paid Beaver Hateman's ransom to the nine people to whom he had sold himself as a slave, though he needn't have troubled to do this, because, as Beaver Hateman said: 'If they want me they have got to fetch me!' He also gave them £9 7s. 6½d. in money. Also they had managed to save some of the Black Tom which had run down from the dump without taking fire.

They had all gathered in a circle, and were having a festival evening.

The dump was still slowly burning, and at about eleven o'clock one or two more kegs caught fire and burned up with a very strong purplish blaze. In the light of it Sigismund Hateman got up to sing. Beaver Hateman appeared to be quite well again, and he was accompanying him on a small guitar.

This is what they were singing. I don't think Uncle heard it, for he had just turned aside to receive one last deputation, but the Old Monkey, listening carefully, heard every word.

> '*I went into the cinema*
> *On a cool and frosty night;*
> *I sat down in the threepenny chair,*
> *And then I got a fright . . .*'

He didn't hear any more, for there were cheers and laughter at this point.

Before Uncle went to bed, he said to the Old Monkey: 'I really think we've finished with Badfort this time.'

The Old Monkey shook his head doubtfully as he went up the stairs.

BADFORT

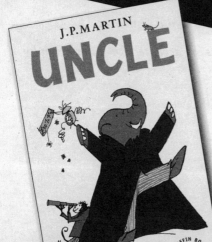

1879   *Born in Scarborough, Yorkshire*

1902   *Becomes a Methodist minister before serving as a
       missionary in South Afritca*

1906   *Marries Nancy Mann in Johannesburg*

1918   *Is an army chaplain in Palestine at the end of the
       First World War*

1934   *His daughter, Stella, and her husband encourage
       him to write down the* Uncle *stories*

1951   *Retired to Timberscombe, Somerset*

1964   *The* Uncle *stories are accepted for publication by
       Jonathan Cape*

1966   *Dies on 24 March*

ABOUT THE ILLUSTRATOR

QUENTIN BLAKE

Quentin Blake is one of Britain's most successful
illustrators. He has illustrated nearly three hundred books
and he was Roald Dahl's favourite illustrator. He has won
many awards, including the Whitbread Award and the
Kate Greenaway Medal, and taught for over twenty years
at the Royal College of Art. In 1999 he became
the first-ever Children's Laureate, and in 2002 he was
awarded the Hans Christian Andersen Award for his
contribution as a children's illustrator – the highest
recognition available to creators of children's books.
In 2013 he was knighted in the New Year's Honours.

WHERE DID THE
STORY COME FROM?

The Uncle *books were first written by J. P. Martin to
entertain his children and grandchildren. First published
in the 1960s and 70s and illustrated by Sir Quentin Blake,
the stories were largely unavailable up until 2016 when*
The Complete Uncle, *containing all six* Uncle *books, was
reissued by Marcus Gipps. This beautiful new edition
contained a wealth of extra material, including articles by
writers Neil Gaiman, Will Self and Kate Summerscale.*

GUESS WHO?

A — He is covered with shaking jelly of a bluish colour, and whenever he is about Uncle looks out for trouble.

B — . . . is almost as rich as Uncle, and far richer than the King of the Badgers.

C — He claims to be a Don, or Spanish gentleman, from Andalusia. He says he lost all his money by speculating in silver foxes; and he's working for Uncle till he gets enough money to retire.
He speaks English with rather a rough accent.

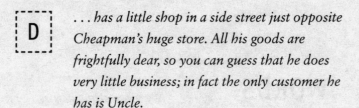

D ... has a little shop in a side street just opposite Cheapman's huge store. All his goods are frightfully dear, so you can guess that he does very little business; in fact the only customer he has is Uncle.

E He loves singing, and he loves being in a tightly packed crowd, because he runs over the heads of the people to the front row.

WORDS GLORIOUS WORDS!

*We often come across **new** or **unfamiliar words** when we're reading. Here are a few unusual words you'll find in this Puffin book. Did you spot any others?*

gramophone *an old-fashioned type of record player*

halfpenny *an old British coin which was worth half a penny*

ironmongery *articles for the house and garden such as tools, nails and pans*

laconic *using very few words, in speech or writing*

noxious *harmful, poisonous or unpleasant*

revolution *a single complete turn (as of a wheel)*

QUIZ

Thinking caps on — let's see how much you can remember! Answers are at the bottom of the next page. (No peeking!)

1 Who gave Uncle a parcel containing a sewing machine, seven pounds of chocolate and a very good brass trumpet?

a) *Old Monkey*

b) *Beaver Hateman*

c) *A waiter*

d) *Cowgill*

2 Who had a big bruise on their forehead that was rapidly disappearing because of Magic Ointment?

a) *Miss Maidy*

b) *Dr Lyre*

c) *Muncle*

d) *Guzman*

3 What year do the boys shout to put Dr Lyre in a good temper?

a) 1606

b) 1529

c) 1238

d) 1066

4 Who turned scarlet and flung a pineapple right at Nailrod Hateman?

a) Miss Wace

b) Uncle

c) Alonzo S. Whitebeard

d) Butterskin Mute

5 What colour is Uncle's dressing-gown?

a) Gold

b) Purple

c) Blue

d) Red

ANSWERS: 1) c 2) a 3) d 4) b 5) b

IN THIS YEAR

1964
Fact Pack

What else was happening in the world when this book was published?

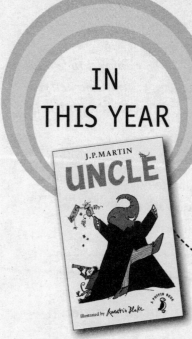

The Summer **Olympics** are held in Tokyo.

Roald Dahl's Charlie and the Chocolate Factory *is first published in the USA.*

The **Labour** party wins the UK general election, with Harold Wilson as prime minister.

Martin Luther King, *leader of the US Civil Rights Movement against racial discrimination, wins the Nobel Peace Prize.*

West Ham United wins the **FA Cup**.

Pop Tarts *are introduced for breakfast!*

MAKE AND DO

Enjoy a nice mug (not bucket!) of cocoa with Uncle!

Cocoa is a drink similar to hot chocolate and it's easy to make, but always ask an adult to help you, especially when heating things up.

YOU WILL NEED:

* 1 tablespoon of cocoa powder
* 1–2 tablespoons of sugar
* A pinch of salt
* 500ml milk
* Some whipped cream and mini marshmallows (for a special treat!)

1 Stir together the cocoa, sugar, salt, and about 2 tablespoons of the milk in a small saucepan over medium-low heat until the cocoa and sugar are dissolved.

2 Carefully add the rest of the milk and heat gently, whisking occasionally, until it is hot, but not boiling.

3 Then pour into a large mug.

4 Top with whipped cream and mini marshmallows and enjoy!

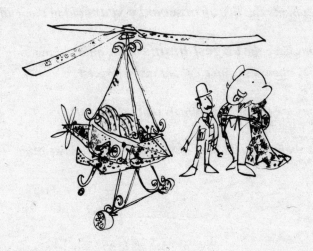

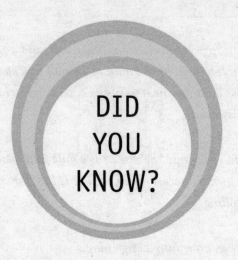

DID YOU KNOW?

Male **elephants** are the largest animals that live on land. They can reach up to four metres in height!

Elephants can live up to **seventy years** old in the wild.

They have the **largest brains** in the animal kingdom. They always say an elephant never forgets!

They are the only mammals that **can't jump**.

Elephants spend about **sixteen hours** a day eating.

PUFFIN
WRITING
TIPS

Watch and read the news and stay tuned to what's happening in the world – you never know what may inspire your next idea.

Write a description of your hometown – as if you were talking to an alien!

Keep a travel journal when you go on a trip so you can capture all the exciting new sights and sounds.